THE
VENADICCI
MARRIAGE
VENGEANCE

THE VENADICCI MARRIAGE VENGEANCE

BY

MELANIE MILBURNE

MILLS & BOON

All the characters in this book have no existence
outside the imagination of the author, and have
no relation whatsoever to anyone bearing the same
name or names. They are not even distantly inspired
by any individual known or unknown to the author,
and all the incidents are pure invention.

All Rights Reserved including the right of
reproduction in whole or in part in any form.
This edition is published by arrangement with
Harlequin Enterprises II BV/S.à.r.l. The text of this
publication or any part thereof may not be reproduced
or transmitted in any form or by any means, electronic
or mechanical, including photocopying, recording,
storage in an information retrieval system, or otherwise,
without the written permission of the publisher.

® and TM are trademarks owned and used by the
trademark owner and/or its licensee. Trademarks
marked with ® are registered with the United Kingdom
Patent Office and/or the Office for Harmonisation in
the Internal Market and in other countries.

First published in Great Britain 2009
Large Print edition 2009
Harlequin Mills & Boon Limited,
Eton House, 18-24 Paradise Road,
Richmond, Surrey TW9 1SR

© Melanie Milburne 2009

ISBN: 978 0 263 20620 3

Set in Times Roman 16½ on 20 pt.
16-0909-51270

Harlequin Mills & Boon policy is to use papers that are
natural, renewable and recyclable products and made
from wood grown in sustainable forests. The logging and
manufacturing process conform to the legal environmental
regulations of the country of origin.

Printed and bound in Great Britain
by CPI Antony Rowe, Chippenham, Wiltshire

To Lorraine Bleasby, Dot Armstrong
and Denise Monks—
my three past and present helpers who free up my time so
I can write. How can I thank you for all you do and have
done for me and my family? This book is dedicated to
you with much love and appreciation. I want the world to
know what truly special women you are.

CHAPTER ONE

'MR VENADICCI has magnanimously offered to squeeze you in between appointments,' the receptionist informed Gabby with crisp, cool politeness. 'But he only has ten minutes available for you.'

Gabby schooled her features into impassivity, even though inside she was fuming and had been for the last hour, as Vinn Venadicci took his time about whether he would respond to her urgent request to see him. 'Thank you,' she said. 'I will try not to take up too much of his precious time.'

No matter how galling it would be to see Vinn again, Gabby determined she would be calm and in control at all times and under all circumstances. Too much was at stake for her to jeopardise things with a show of temper or a tirade of insults, as she would have done without hesitation seven years ago. A lot of water had flowed under the bridge since then, but she was not going to tell him just how dirty some of it had been. That would be conceding defeat, and in spite of everything that had happened she wasn't quite ready to shelve all of her pride where Vinn Venadicci was concerned.

His plush suite of offices in the heart of the financial district in Sydney was a reflection of his meteoric rise to fame in the property investment industry. From his humble beginnings as the born-out-of-wedlock bad-boy son of the St Clair family's Italian-born house-cleaner Rose, he had surprised everyone—except Gabby's father, who had always seen Vinn's potential and had done what he could to give him the leg-up he needed.

Thinking of her father was just the boost to her resolve Gabby needed right now. Henry St Clair was in frail health after a serious heart attack, which meant a lot of the responsibility to keep things running smoothly while he went through the arduous process of triple bypass surgery and rehabilitation had fallen on her shoulders, with her mother standing stalwartly and rather stoically by her father's side.

This hiccup to do with the family business had come out of the blue—and if her father got wind of it, it was just the thing that could set off another heart attack. Gabby would walk across hot coals to avoid that—even meet face to face with Vinn Venadicci.

She raised her hand to the door marked with Vinn's name and gave it a quick two-hit tattoo, her stomach twisting with the prickly sensation she always felt when she was within striking distance of him.

'Come.'

She straightened her shoulders and opened the door, her chin at a proud height as she took the ridiculously long journey to his desk, where he was seated. That he didn't rise to his feet was the sort of veiled insult she more or less expected from him. He had always had an insolent air about him, even when he had lived on and off with his mother, in a servants' cottage at the St Clair Point Piper mansion.

In that nanosecond before he spoke Gabby quickly drank in his image, her heart giving a little jerk inside her chest in spite of all of her efforts to control it. Even when he was seated his height was intimidating, and the black raven's wing of his hair caught the light coming in from the windows, giving it a glossy sheen that made her fingers itch to reach out and touch it. His nose was crooked from one too many of the brawls he had been involved in during his youth, but—unlike many other high-profile business-men, who would have sought surgical correction by now—Vinn wore his war wounds like a medal. Just like the scar that interrupted his left eyebrow, giving him a dangerous don't-mess-with-me look that was disturbingly attractive.

'So how is the Merry Widow?' he said with a mocking glint in his eyes as they ran over her lazily. 'Long time no see. What is it now…? One year or is it two? You look like grief suits you, Gabriella. I have never seen you looking more beautiful.'

Gabby felt her spine go rigid at his sardonic taunt. Tristan Glendenning had been dead for just over two years, and yet Vinn never failed to refer to him in that unmistakably scathing manner whenever their paths crossed. She felt each and every reference to her late husband like a hard slap across the face—not that she would ever admit that to Vinn.

She pulled her temper back into line with an effort. 'May I sit down?'

He waved a hand in a careless manner. 'Put your cute little bottom down on that chair. But only for ten minutes,' he said. 'I have back-to-back commitments today.'

Gabby sat down on the edge of the chair, hating that his words had summoned such a hot flush to her cheeks. He had the most annoying habit of unnerving her with personal comments that made her aware of her body in a way no one else could.

'So,' he said, leaning back in his chair with a squeak of very expensive leather, 'what can I do for you, Gabriella?'

She silently ground her teeth. No one else called her by her full name. Only him. She knew he did it deliberately. He had done it since she was fourteen, when his mother had been hired as the resident cleaner, bringing her brooding eighteen-year-old son with her. Although Gabby had to grudgingly admit that the way he said her name was quite unlike anyone else. He had been born in Australia but, because he had been fluent in Italian from a very young age, he made her name sound faintly foreign and exotic. The four distinct syllables coming out of his sensually sculptured mouth always made the hairs on the back of her neck stand to attention like tiny soldiers.

'I am here to discuss a little problem that's come up,' she said, hoping he couldn't see how she was tying her hands into knots in her lap. 'With my father out of action at present, I would appreciate your advice on how to handle it.'

He sat watching her in that musing way of his, clicking and releasing his gold ballpoint pen with meticulously timed precision: on, off, on, off, as if he was timing his own slow and steady heartbeat.

'How is your father this morning?' he asked. 'I saw him last night in Intensive Care. He was looking a little worse for wear, but that's to be expected, I suppose.'

Gabby was well aware of Vinn's regular visits to her father's bedside, and had deliberately avoided being there at the same time. 'He's doing OK,' she said. 'His surgery is scheduled for some time next week. I think they've been waiting for him to stabilise first.'

'Yes, of course,' he said putting the pen to one side. 'But the doctors are hopeful of a full recovery, are they not?'

Gabby tried not to look at his hands, but for some reason her eyes drifted back to where they were now lying palm down on the smoothly polished desk. He had broad, square-shaped hands, with long fingers, and the dusting of masculine hair was enough to remind her of his virility as a full-blooded male of thirty-two.

He was no longer the youth of the past. His skin was clear and cleanly shaven, and at six foot four he carried not a gram of excess flesh; every toned and taut muscle spoke of his punishing physical regime. It made Gabby's ad hoc attempts at regular exercise with a set of free weights and a home DVD look rather pathetic in comparison.

'Gabriella?'

Gabby gave herself a mental shake and dragged her eyes back to his. He had such amazing eyes. And his ink-black hair and deeply olive skin made the smoky grey colour of them all the more striking.

She had never been told the details of his father, and she had never really bothered to ask Vinn directly—although she assumed his father wasn't Italian, like his mother. Gabby had heard one or two whispers as she was growing up, which had seemed to suggest Vinn's mother found the subject painful and refused ever to speak of it.

'Um…I'm not really sure,' she said, in answer to his question regarding her father's recovery. 'I haven't really spoken with his doctors.'

As soon as she said the words she realised how disengaged and uncaring they made her sound— as if her father's health was not a top priority for her, when nothing could be further from the truth. She wouldn't be here now if it wasn't for her love and concern for both of her parents. She would never have dreamed of asking for Vinn's help if desperation hadn't shoved her head-first through his door.

'I take it this unprecedented visit to my lair is about the takeover bid for the St Clair Island Resort?' he said into the ringing silence.

Gabby had trouble disguising her reaction. She had only just become aware of it herself. How on earth had he found out about it?

'Um…yes, it is actually,' she said, shifting restlessly in her seat. 'As you probably know, my

father took out a substantial loan for the refurbishment of the resort about a year and a half
ago. But late yesterday I was informed there's
been a call. If we don't pay the loan back the
takeover bid will go through uncontested. I can't
allow that to happen.'

'Have you spoken to your accountants about
it?' he asked.

Gabby felt another layer of her professional
armour dissolve without trace. 'They said there
is no way that amount of money can be raised in
twenty-four hours,' she said, lowering her gaze
a fraction.

He began his on-off click with his pen once more,
a little faster now, as if in time with his sharp intelligence as he mulled over what strategy to adopt.

'I don't suppose you've mentioned it to your
father,' he said, phrasing it as neither a question
nor a statement.

'No…' she said, still not quite able to hold his
gaze. 'I didn't want to stress him. I'm frightened
the news could trigger another heart attack.'

'What about the on-site resort managers?' he asked. 'Do they know anything about this?'

Gabby rolled her lips together as she brought her gaze back to his. 'I spoke to Judy and Garry Foster last night. They are concerned for their jobs, of course, but I tried to reassure them I would sort things out this end.'

'Have you brought all the relevant documentation with you?' he asked after a short pause.

'Um…no… I thought I would run it by you first.' Gabby knew it was the wrong answer. She could see it in his incisive grey-blue eyes as they quietly assessed her.

She felt so incompetent—like a child playing with oversized clothes in a dress-up box. The shoes she had put on were too big. She had always known it, but hadn't had the courage to say it out loud to her parents, who had held such high hopes for her after her older brother Blair's tragic death. The giant hole he had left in their lives had made her all the more determined to fill in where she could. But she still felt as if the shoes were too big, too ungainly for her—even though she had trudged in them with gritted teeth for the last seven and a half years.

Vinn leaned back in his seat, his eyes still centred on hers. 'So you have less than twenty-four hours to come up with the funds otherwise the takeover bid goes through unchallenged?' he summated.

Gabby ran the tip of her tongue across lips dryer than ancient parchment. 'That's right,' she said, doing her level best to quell her dread at the thought of such an outcome. 'If it goes through our family will be left with only a thirty-five percent share in the resort. I'm not sure what you can do, but I know my father. If he wasn't so unwell he would probably have run it by you first, to see if there's anything we can do to avoid losing the major sharehold.'

His eyes were still locked on hers, unblinking almost, which unsettled Gabby more than she wanted it to.

'Do you know who is behind the takeover?' he asked.

She shook her head and allowed a tiny sigh to escape. 'I've asked around, but no one seems to know anything about the company that's behind it.'

'How much is the margin call?'

Gabby took an uneven breath, her stomach feeling as if a nest of hungry bull ants were eating their way out. 'Two point four million dollars.'

His dark brows lifted a fraction. 'Not exactly an amount you would have sitting around in petty cash,' he commented wryly.

'It's not an amount that is sitting *anywhere* in any of the St Clair accounts,' she said, running her tongue over her lips again, as if to wipe away the residue of panic that seemed to have permanently settled there. 'I'm sure my father never expected anything like this to happen—or at least not before we had time to recoup on the investment. The markets have been unstable for several months now. We wouldn't be the first to have redeveloped at the wrong time.'

'True.'

Gabby shifted in her chair again. 'So…I was

wondering what you suggest we do…' She sucked in a tiny breath, her heart thumping so loudly she could feel a roaring in her ears. 'I…I know it's a bit of an imposition, but my father respects your judgment. That's basically why I am here.'

Vinn gave a deep and utterly masculine rumble of laughter. 'Yes, well, I can't imagine you pressing for an audience with me to share your observations on the day's weather,' he said. And then, with a little sneering quirk of his mouth, he added, 'You have five minutes left, by the way.'

Gabby pursed her lips as she fought her temper down. 'I think you know what I'm asking you to do,' she said tightly. 'Don't make me spell it out just to bolster your already monumental ego.'

A flicker of heat made his eyes look like the centre of a flame as he leaned forward across the desk. 'You want me to pay off the loan, is that it?' he said, searing her gaze with his.

'My father has done a lot for you—' she launched into the speech she had hastily prepared in the middle of the night '—he paid bail for that stolen car charge you were on when you were eighteen, not long after you came to live with us. And he gave you your very first loan for university. You wouldn't be where you are today without his mentorship and his belief in you.'

He leaned back in his chair, his demeanour casual as you please. He picked up his pen again, but this time rolled it between two of his long fingers. 'Two point four million dollars is a lot of money, Gabriella,' he said. 'If I were to hand over such an amount I would want something in return. Something I could depend on to cover my losses if things were to take a sudden downturn.'

Gabby felt a prickle of alarm lift the surface of her skin. 'You mean like a guarantee or something?' she asked. 'W-we can have something drawn up with the lawyers. A repayment plan over…say five years, with fixed interest. How does that sound?'

He gave a smile that wasn't reflected in those unreadable eyes of his. 'It sounds risky,' he said.

'I would want a better guarantee than something written on paper.'

She looked at him in confusion. 'I'm not sure what you mean… Are you asking for more collateral? There's the house but Mum and Dad will need somewhere to—'

'I don't want their house,' he said, his eyes still burning like fire into hers.

Gabby ran her tongue over her lips again, her stomach doing another nervous shuffling movement. 'Then…then what do you want?' she asked, annoyed with herself at how whispery and frightened her voice sounded.

The silence became charged with something she couldn't quite identify. The air was thick—so thick she could scarcely breathe without feeling as if her chest was being pressed down with a weight far too heavy for her finely boned ribcage. Apprehension slowly but stealthily crept up her spine, with tiptoeing, ice-cold steps, disturbing each and every fine hair on the back of her neck.

Vinn's eyes were fathomless pools of murky

shadows as they held onto hers. 'How do you feel about stepping up to the plate as guarantor?' he asked.

Gabby frowned. 'I don't have anything like that amount at my disposal,' she said, her heart starting to race. 'I have a small income I draw from the company for my immediate needs, but nothing that would cover that amount at short notice.'

He tilted one of his dark brows ironically. 'So I take it your late husband didn't leave you in the manner to which you have been accustomed for all of your silver-spooned life?' he said.

Gabby lowered her gaze and looked at her knotted hands rather than see the I-told-you-so gleam in his eyes. 'Tristan's finances were in a bit of a mess when he died so suddenly. There were debts and…so many things to see to…' *And so many secrets to keep*, she thought grimly.

A three-beat pause passed.

'I will give you the money,' Vinn said at last. 'I can have it in your father's business account with a few clicks of my computer mouse. Your little problem will be solved before you catch the lift down to the ground floor of this building.'

Gabby could sense a 'but' coming, and waited with bated breath for him to deliver it. She knew him too well to expect him to hand over that amount of money without some sort of condition on the deal. Sure, he admired and respected her father, he even tolerated her mother to some degree, but he had every reason to hate Gabby, and she couldn't imagine him missing a golden opportunity like this to demonstrate how deep his loathing of her ran.

'But of course there will be some conditions on the deal,' he inserted into the silence.

Gabby felt her heart skip a beat when she saw the determined glint in his gaze. 'W-what sort of conditions?' she asked.

'I am surprised you haven't already guessed,' he remarked, with an inscrutable smile playing with the sensual line of his mouth, giving him a devilishly ruthless look.

Gabby felt another shiver of apprehension pass

through her. 'I—I have no idea what you're talking about,' she said, her nails scoring into her palms as she tightened her fists in her lap.

'Ah, but I think you do,' he said. 'Remember the night before your wedding?'

She forced herself to hold his gaze, even though she could feel a bloom of guilty colour staining her cheeks. The memory was as clear as if it had happened yesterday. God knew she had relived that brief, fiery exchange so many times during her train wreck of a marriage, wondering how different her life might have been if she had heeded Vinn's warning…

The wedding rehearsal had been going ahead, in spite of Tristan calling at the last minute to say he had been held up in a meeting and might not make it after all, and Vinn had arrived at the church bleary-eyed and unshaven from an international flight, after spending the last six months in Italy where his terminally ill mother had asked to be taken to die.

He had leaned in that indolent way of his

against one of the columns at the back of the cathedral, his strong arms folded, one ankle crossed over the other, and his eyes—those amazingly penetrating eyes—every time Gabby happened to glance his way, trained on her.

Once the minister had taken them through their paces, Gabby's mother had invited everyone present back to the St Clair house for a light supper. Gabby had secretly hoped Vinn would decline the invitation, but as she had come out of one of the upstairs bathrooms half an hour or so later, Vinn had stepped forward to block her path.

'I'd like a word with you, Gabriella,' he said. 'In private.'

'I can't imagine what you'd have to say to me,' she said coldly, as she tried to sidestep him, but he took one of her wrists in the steel bracelet of his fingers, the physical contact sending sparks of fizzing electricity up and down her arm. 'Let me go, Vinn,' she said, trying to pull away.

His hold tightened to the point of pain. 'Don't go through with it, Gabriella,' he said in a strained sort of tone she had never heard him use before. 'He's not the right man for you.'

Pride made her put her chin up. 'Let me go,' she repeated, and, using her free hand, scraped the back of his hand with her nails.

He captured her other hand and pulled her up close—closer than she had ever been to him before. It was a shock to find how hard the wall of his chest was, and the latent power of his thighs pressed against her trembling body made her spine feel loose and watery all of a sudden.

His eyes were burning as they warred with hers. 'Call it off,' he said. 'Your parents will understand. It's not too late.'

She threw him an icy glare. 'If you don't let me go this instant I'll tell everyone you tried to assault me. You'll go to jail. Tristan's father will act for me in court. You won't have a leg to stand on.'

His mouth tightened, and she saw a pulse beating like a drum in his neck. 'Glendenning is only marrying you for your money,' he ground out.

Gabby was incensed, even though a tiny pinhole of doubt had already worn through the thick veil of denial she had stitched in place over the last few weeks of her engagement. 'You don't know what you're talking about,' she spat at him. 'Tristan loves me. I know he does.'

Vinn's hands were like handcuffs on her wrists. 'If it's marriage you want, then marry me. At least you'll know what you're getting.'

Gabby laughed in his face. 'Marry *you?*' She injected as much insult as she could into her tone. 'And spend the rest of my life like your mother did, scrubbing other people's houses? Thanks, but no thanks.'

'I won't let you go through with it, Gabriella,' he warned. 'If you don't call the wedding off tonight I will stand up during the ceremony tomorrow and tell the congregation why the marriage should not go ahead.'

'You wouldn't dare!'

His eyes challenged hers. 'You just watch me, Blondie,' he said. 'Do you want the whole of

Sydney to know what sort of man you are marrying?'

She threw him a look of pure venom. 'I am going to make damned sure you're not even *at* my wedding,' she spat back at him. 'I'm going to speak to the security firm Dad has organised and have you banned from entry. I'm marrying Tristan tomorrow no matter what you say. I love him.'

'You don't know who or what you want right now,' he said, with a fast-beating pulse showing at the corner of his mouth. 'Damn it, Gabriella, you're only just twenty-one. Your brother's suicide has thrown you. It's thrown all of us. Your engagement was a knee-jerk reaction. For God's sake, a blind man could see it.'

The mention of her brother and his tragic death unleashed a spurt of anger Gabby had not been able to express out of respect for her shattered parents. It rose inside her like an explosion of lava, and with the sort of strength she had no idea she possessed, she tore herself out of his hold and delivered a stinging slap to his stubbly jaw. It must have hurt him, for her hand began to throb unbearably, all the delicate bones feeling as if they had been crushed by a house brick.

Time stood still for several heart-stopping seconds.

Something dangerous flickered in his grey-blue eyes, and then with a speed that knocked the breath right out of her lungs he pulled her into his crushing embrace, his hot, angry mouth coming down on hers...

Gabby had to shake herself back to the present. She hated thinking about that kiss. She hated re-membering how she had so shamelessly re-sponded to it. And she hated recalling the bracelet of fingertip bruises she had worn on her wedding day—as if Vinn Venadicci, in spite of her covert word to Security to keep him out of the church, had vicariously come along to mock her marriage to Tristan Glendenning anyway.

'Just tell me what you want and get it over with,' she said now, with a flash of irritation, as she continued to face him combatively across the expanse of his desk.

'I want you to be my wife.'

Gabby wasn't sure what shocked her the most: the blunt statement of his intentions or the terrifying realisation she had no choice but to agree.

'That seems rather an unusual request, given the fact we hate each other and have always done so,' she managed to say, without—she hoped—betraying the flutter of her heart.

'You don't hate me, Gabriella,' he said with a sardonic smile. 'You just hate how I make you feel. It's always been there between us, has it not? The forbidden fruit of attraction: the rich heiress and the bad boy servant's son. A potent mix, don't you think?'

Gabby sent him a withering look. 'You are delusional, Vinn,' she said. 'I have never given you any encouragement to think anything but how much I detest you.'

He got to his feet and, glancing at his designer

watch, informed her dispassionately, 'Time's up, Blondie.'

She gritted her teeth. 'I need more time to consider your offer,' she bit out.

'The offer is closing in less than thirty seconds,' he said with an indomitable look. 'Take or leave it.'

Frustration pushed Gabby to her feet. 'This is my father's life's work we're talking about here,' she said, her voice rising to an almost shrill level. 'He built up the St Clair Resort from scratch after that cyclone in the seventies. How can you turn your back on him after all he's done for you? Damn it, Vinn. You would be pacing the exercise yard at Pentridge Jail if it wasn't for what our family has done for you.'

His eyes were diamond-hard, the set to his mouth like carved granite. 'That is my price, Gabriella,' he said. 'Marriage or nothing.'

She clenched her hands into fists, her whole body shaking with impotent rage. 'You know I can't say no. You know it and you want to rub it in. You're only doing this because I rejected your stupid spur of the moment proposal seven years ago.'

He leaned towards the intercom on his desk and pressing the button, said calmly, 'Rachel? Is my next client here? Mrs Glendenning is just leaving.'

Gabby could see her father's hard-earned business slipping out of his control. He would have to sell the house—the house his parents and grandparents before him had lived in. Gabby could imagine the crushing disappointment etched on his face when she told him she had failed him, that she hadn't been able to keep things afloat as her brilliantly talented brother would have done. If Blair was still alive he would have networked and found someone to tide him over by now. He would have had that margin call solved with a quick call to one of his well-connected mates. That was the way he had worked. He had lived on the adrenalin rush of life while she… Well, that was the problem.

She couldn't cope.

She liked to know what was going to happen

and when it was going to happen. She hated the cut and thrust of business, the endless going-nowhere meetings, the tedious networking at corporate functions—not to mention the reams of pointless paperwork. And most of all she hated the rows and rows of numbers that seemed more of a blur to her than anything else.

Gabby liked to… Well, there was no point in thinking about what she liked to do, because it just wasn't going to happen. Her dreams had had to be shelved and would remain shelved—at least until her father could take up the reins again… *If* he took up the reins again, she thought, with another deep quiver of panic.

Gabby had been the last person to speak to her brother; the last person to see him alive before he ended his life with a drug overdose. Because of that she had responsibilities to face. And face them she would. Even if they were totally repugnant to her. Being forced to marry a man like Vinn Venadicci was right up there on the repugnant scale. Or maybe repugnant wasn't quite the right word, she grudgingly conceded. Vinn was hardly what any woman would describe as physically off-putting. He was downright gorgeous, when it came down to it. That long, leanly muscled frame, that silky black hair, those sensually sculptured lips and those mesmerising eyes were enough to send any woman's heart aflutter—and Gabby's was doing a whole lot more than fluttering right now at the thought of being formally tied to him.

Entering into a marriage contract with Vinn was asking for trouble—but what else could she do? Who was going to lend her that amount of money in less than twenty-four hours?

Gabby gulped as she glanced at him again. Could she do it? Could she agree to marry him even though it was madness?

Actually, it was dangerous… Yes, that was the word she had been looking for. Vinn was dangerous. He was arrogant, he was a playboy, and—even more disturbing—he had a chip on his shoulder where she was concerned.

But she had nowhere else to turn—no other solution to fix this within the narrow timeframe. It was up to her to save her family's business, even if it meant agreeing to his preposterous conditions.

'All right,' Gabby said on a whooshing breath of resignation. 'I'll do it.'

'Fine,' Vinn said, in a tone that suggested he had never had any doubt of her accepting, which somehow made it all the more galling. 'The money will be deposited within the next few minutes. I will pick you up this evening for dinner, so we can go through the wedding arrangements.'

Gabby felt herself quake with alarm. 'Couldn't we just wait a few days until I have time to—?'

His cynical laugh cut her off. 'Until you have time to think of a way out, eh, Gabriella? I don't think so, *cara*. Now I have you I am not going to let you escape.'

'What am I supposed to say to my parents?' she asked, scowling at him even as her stomach did another nosedive of dread.

He smiled. 'Why not tell them you've finally come to your senses and agreed to marry me?'

She gave him another glare that would have stripped three decades of paint off a wall. 'They will think I have taken leave of my senses.'

'Or they will think you have fallen head over heels in love,' he said. 'Which is exactly what I would prefer them to believe at this point in time. Your father's health is unstable and will be for some weeks after the surgery, I imagine. I wouldn't want him to suffer a relapse out of concern for you or for his business.'

Gabby couldn't argue with that, but she resented him using it as a lever to get her to fall meekly in with his plans. 'I was planning on going to the hospital this evening,' she said tightly. 'Will I meet you there or at the house?'

'I have a couple of meetings that might string out, so if I don't make it to the hospital I will meet you at the house around eight-thirty,' he said. 'I would like to speak to your father at some point about my intentions.'

Gabby couldn't stop her top lip from curling. 'Somehow you don't strike me as the traditional type, asking a girl's father for her hand in marriage. In fact I didn't think you were the marrying type at all. All we ever read about you in the press is how you move from one relationship to another within a matter of weeks.'

He gave her another unreadable smile. 'Variety, as they say, is the spice of life,' he said. 'But even the most restless man eventually feels the need to put down some roots.'

She eyed him warily. 'This marriage between us…it's not for the long term…is it?'

'Only for as long as it achieves its aim,' he said—which Gabby realised hadn't really answered her question.

Vinn moved past her to hold the door open for her. 'I will see you tonight,' he said. 'I'll call you if I am going to be late.'

She brushed past him, her head at a proud angle. The subtle notes of her perfume danced around his face, making his nostrils flare involuntarily. She smelt of orange blossom. Or was it honeysuckle? He couldn't quite tell. Maybe it was both. That was the thing about Gabriella—she was a combination of so many things, any one of them alone was enough to send his senses spinning. But all of them put together? Well, that was half his problem, wasn't it?

The door clicked shut behind her and Vinn released the breath he'd unconsciously been holding. 'Damn,' he said, raking a hand through his hair. 'God damn it to hell.'

'Mr Venadicci?' His receptionist's cool, crisp voice sounded over the intercom. 'Mr Winchester is here now. Shall I send him in?'

Vinn pulled in an uneven breath and released it just as raggedly. 'Yeah…' he said, dropping his hand by his side. 'I'll see him. But tell him I've only got five minutes.'

CHAPTER TWO

GABBY put on her bravest face while she visited her father's bedside. The tubes and heart monitor leads attached to his grey-tinged body made her stomach churn with anguish—the very same anguish she could see played out on her mother's face.

'How are you, Dad?' she whispered softly as she bent down to kiss his cheek.

'Still alive and kicking,' he said, and even managed a lopsided grin, but Gabby could see the worry and fear in his whisky-coloured eyes.

'Have the doctors told you anything more?' she asked, addressing both her mother and father.

'The surgery is being brought forward to tomorrow,' Pamela St Clair answered. 'Vinn spoke to the cardiac surgeon and organised it when he was here earlier. He insisted your father's case be made a priority. You just missed him, actually. It's a wonder you didn't pass him in the corridor.'

Gabby stiffened. 'Vinn was here just now?'

'Yes, dear,' her mother said. 'He's been here every day. But you know that.'

'Yes… It's just I was speaking to him this morning and he said he had meetings to attend all afternoon and evening,' she said, unconsciously biting her lip.

Her mother gave her a searching look. 'I hope you're not going to be difficult about Vinn,' she said, with a hint of reproof in her tone. 'He's been nothing but supportive, and the least you could do is be civil towards him—especially now.'

Gabby could have laughed out loud at the irony of her mother's turnaround. Pamela St Clair had always been of the old school, that actively discouraged fraternisation with any of the household staff. She had barely spoken to Vinn's mother during the years Rose had worked at the

St Clair estate other than to hand Rose a long list of menial tasks to get through. She had been even less friendly towards Rose's surly son during the short time he had lived there with his mother. And after he'd had that slight run-in with the law Pamela had tried to ban him from the property altogether, but Gabby's father had insisted Vinn be allowed to visit his mother as usual.

Gabby hadn't been much better towards Rose—which was something she had come to sincerely regret in the years since. She still cringed in shame at how inconsiderate she had been at times, carelessly leaving her things about, without a care for the person who had to come along behind her and pick them up.

But it was Gabby's treatment of Vinn that had been the most unforgivable. She had been absolutely appalling to him for most of her teenage years—teasing him in front of her giggling friends, talking about him in disparaging terms well within his hearing. She had flirted with him, and then turned her nose up at him with disgraceful regularity. She had no excuse for her behaviour other than that she had been an insecure teenager, privately struggling with body issues, who, in an effort to build her self-esteem, had tended to mix with a rather shallow crowd of rich-kid friends who had not learned to respect people from less affluent backgrounds.

On one distressingly memorable occasion, at the urging of her troublemaking friends, Gabby had left an outrageously seductive note for Vinn, asking him to meet her in the summerhouse that evening. But instead of turning up she had watched from one of the top windows of the mansion, laughing with her friends at how he had arrived at the summerhouse with a bunch of white roses for her. What had shamed her most had been Vinn's reaction. Instead of bawling her out, calling her any one of the despicable names she had no doubt deserved, he had said nothing. Not to her, not to her parents, and not even to her brother Blair, whom he'd spent most of his spare time with whenever he had visited the estate.

Gabby's father reached out a weak hand towards her, the slight tremble of his touch bringing her back to the present. 'Vinn is a good man,' he said. 'I know you're still grieving the loss of Tristan, but I think you should seriously consider his proposal. You could do a lot worse. I know he's had a bit of a rough start, but he's done well for himself. No one could argue with that. I always knew he had the will-power and the drive to make it once he got on the right path. I'm glad he has chosen you as his bride. He will look after you well. I know he will.'

Gabby couldn't quite disguise her surprise that Vinn had already spoken to her father. She moistened her dry lips and tried on a bright smile, but it didn't feel comfortable on her mouth. 'So he's spoken to you about our…relationship?'

Her father smiled. 'I gave him my full blessing, Gabby. I must say I wasn't the least surprised to hear the news of your engagement.'

Gabby frowned. 'You…you weren't?

He shook his head and gave her hand another light squeeze. 'You've been striking sparks off each other since you were a teenager,' he said. 'For a time there I thought… Well…Blair's accident changed everything, of course.'

Gabby felt the familiar frustration that neither of her parents had ever accepted their only son's death as suicide. They still refused to acknowledge he had been dabbling with drugs—but then stubborn denial was a St Clair trait, and she had her own fair share of it.

'I'm glad you both approve,' she said, banking down her emotion. 'We are having dinner this evening to discuss the wedding arrangements.'

'Yes, he told us it wasn't going to be a grand affair,' her mother said. 'I think that's wise, under the circumstances. After all, it's your second marriage. It seems pointless going to the same fuss as last time.'

Gabby couldn't agree more. The amount of money spent on her marriage to Tristan Glendenning had been such a waste when within hours of the ceremony and lavish reception she had realised the terrible mistake she had made.

She stretched her mouth into another staged smile and reached across to kiss both her parents. 'I'd better get going,' she said, readjusting her handbag over her shoulder. 'Is there anything you need before I go?'

'No, dear,' her mother assured her. 'Vinn brought some fruit and a couple of novels for your father to read by that author he enjoys so much. I must say Vinn's grown into a perfect gentleman. Your father is right. You could do a lot worse—especially as you're a widow. Not many men want a woman someone else has had, so to speak.'

Gabby silently ground her teeth. If only her mother knew the truth about her ill-fated first marriage. 'I'll see you tomorrow,' she said, and with another unnatural smile left.

The St Clair mansion was situated on the water-front in the premier harbourside suburb of Point Piper, flanked on either side by equally luxuri-ous homes for the super-rich and famous. The views across Sydney Harbour were spectacular, and the house and grounds offered a lifestyle that was decadent to say the least.

Gabby had moved back home two years ago, after Tristan's death in a car accident, and although now and again she had toyed with the idea of finding a place of her own, so far she had done nothing about doing so. The mansion was big enough for her to have the privacy she needed, and with her finances still on the shaky side, after the trail of debts her late husband had left behind, she had decided to leave things as they were for the time being.

The doorbell sounded right on the stroke of eight-thirty and Gabby was still not ready. Her straight ash-blonde hair was in heated rollers, to give it some much needed body, and she was still in her bathrobe after a shower.

She wriggled into a black sheath of a designer dress she'd had for years, and shoved her feet into three inch heels, all the time trying not to panic as another minute passed. She slashed some lipstick across her mouth and dusted her cheeks with translucent powder, giving her lashes a quick brush with a mascara wand before tugging at the rollers. Her hair cascaded around her shoulders in springy waves, and with a quick brush she was ready—or at least as ready as she could be under the circumstances. Which wasn't saying much…

Vinn checked his watch and wondered if he should use the key Henry had insisted he keep on him at all times. But just as he was searching for it on his keyring the door opened and Gabriella was standing there, looking as if she had just stepped off the catwalk. Her perfume drifted towards him, an exotic blend of summer blooms. Her normally straight hair was bouncing freely around her bare shoulders, the black halter neck dress showing off her slim figure to maximum advantage.

It had always amazed him how someone so slim could have such generous breasts without having to resort to any sort of enhancement. The tempting shadow of her cleavage drew his eyes like a magnet, and he had to fight to keep his eyes on her toffee-brown ones. She had made them all the more noticeable with the clever use of smoky eyeshadow and eyeliner, and her full and sensual lips were a glossy pink which was the same shade as that on her fingernails.

'I'll just get my wrap and purse,' she said, leaving the door open.

Vinn watched her walk over the marbled floor of the expansive foyer on killer heels, one of her hands adjusting her earrings before she scooped up a purse and silky wrap. She turned and came back towards him, her chin at the haughty angle he had always associated with her—even when she was a sulky fourteen-year-old, with braces on her teeth and puppy fat on her body.

'Shall we get this over with?' she said, as if they were about to face a hangman.

Vinn had to suppress his desire to make her eat her carelessly slung words. She meant to insult him, and would no doubt do so at every opportunity, but he had the upper hand now and she would have to toe the line. It would bring him immense pleasure to tame her—especially after what her fiancé had done to him on the day of their wedding on her behalf. The scar over his left eyebrow was a permanent reminder of what lengths she would go to in order to have her way. But things were going to be done his way this time around, and the sooner she got used to it the better.

He led the way to his car and opened the passenger door for her, closing it once she was inside with the seatbelt in place. He waited until they were heading towards the city before he spoke.

'Your parents were surprisingly positive about our decision to marry—your mother in particular. I was expecting her to drop into a faint at the thought of her daughter hooking up with a fatherless foreigner, but she practically gushed in gratefulness that someone had put up their hand to scoop you off the shelf, so to speak.'

Gabby sent him a brittle look. 'Must you be so

insulting?' she asked. 'And by the way—not that I'm splitting hairs or anything—but it wasn't exactly *our* plan to get married, it was yours.'

He gave an indifferent lift of one shoulder. 'There is no point arguing about the terms now the margin call has been dealt with,' he said. 'I have always had a lot of time for your father, but your mother has always been an out-and-out snob who thinks the measure of a man is what's in his wallet.'

'Yes, well, it's practically the only thing you've got going for *you*,' she shot back with a scowl.

He laughed as he changed gears. 'What's in my wallet has just got you and your family out of a trainload of trouble, *cara,* so don't go insulting me, hmm? I might take it upon myself to withdraw my support—and then where will you be?'

Gabby turned her head away, looking almost sightlessly at the silvery skyscrapers of the city as they flashed past. He was right of course. She would have to curb her tongue, otherwise he might renege on the deal. It would be just the kind of thing he would do, and relish every moment of doing it. Although it went against everything she believed in to pander to a man she loathed with every gram of her being, she really didn't see she had any choice in the matter. Vinn had the power to make or break her; she had to remember that.

She had never thought it was possible to hate someone so much. Her blood was thundering through her veins with the sheer force of it. He was so arrogant, so very self-assured. Against all the odds he had risen above his impoverished background and was using his new-found power to control her. But she was not going to give in without a fight. He might make her his wife, but it would be in name only.

Not that she would tell him just yet, of course. That would be the card up her sleeve she would reveal only once the ceremony was over. Vinn would be in for a surprise to find his new wife was not prepared to sleep with him. She would be a trophy wife—a gracious hostess, who would say the right things in the right places, and smile and act the role of the devoted partner in public if needed—but in private she would be the same Gabby who had left the score of her nails on the back of his hand the night before her wedding.

The restaurant he had booked was on the waterfront, and the night-time view over the harbour was even more stunning, with the twinkling of lights from the various tour ferries and floating restaurants. The evening air was sultry and warm, heavy with humidity, as if there was a storm brewing in the atmosphere.

Gabby walked stiffly by Vinn's side, suffering the light touch of his hand beneath her elbow as he escorted her inside the award-winning restaurant. The head waiter greeted Vinn with deference, before leading the way to a table in a prime position overlooking the fabulous views.

'Have you ever dined here before?' Vinn asked, once they were seated and their starched napkins were expertly draped over their laps.

Gabby shook her head and glanced at the

drinks menu. 'No, I haven't been out all that much lately.'

'Have you dated anyone since your husband died?' he asked, with what appeared to be only casual interest.

She still looked at the menu rather than face his gaze. 'It's only been two years,' she said curtly. 'I'm in no hurry.'

'Do you miss him?'

Gabby put the menu down and looked at Vinn in irritation. 'What sort of a question is that?' she asked. 'We were married for five years.' *Five miserably unhappy years.* But she could hardly tell him that. She hadn't even told her parents.

She hadn't told anyone. Who was there to tell? She had never been particularly good at friendships; her few girlfriends had found Tristan boorish and overbearing, and each of them had gradually moved on, with barely an e-mail or a text to see how she was doing. Gabby knew it was mostly her fault for constantly covering for her husband's inadequacies. She had become

what the experts called an enabler, a co-
dependant. Tristan had been allowed to get away
with his unspeakable behaviour because she had
not been able to face the shame of facing up to
the mistake she had made in marrying him. As
a result she had become an adept liar, and,
although it was painful to face it, she knew she
had only herself to blame.

'You didn't have children,' Vinn inserted into
the silence. 'Was that your choice or his?'

'It wasn't something we got around to discuss-
ing,' she said, as she inspected the food menu
with fierce concentration.

The waiter came and took their order for
drinks. Gabby chose a very rich cocktail—more
for Dutch courage than anything. It was what she
felt she needed just now: a thick fog of alcohol
to survive an evening in Vinn's company.

Vinn, on the other hand, ordered a tall glass of
iced mineral water—a well-known Italian brand,
she noticed.

'You'd better go easy on that drink of yours,

Gabriella,' he cautioned as she took a generous mouthful. 'Drinking on an empty stomach is not wise. Alcohol has a well-known disinhibitory effect on behaviour. You might find yourself doing things you wouldn't normally do.'

She gave him a haughty look. 'You mean like enjoying your company instead of loathing every minute of it?'

His grey-blue eyes gave a flame-like flash. 'You will enjoy a whole lot more than just my company before the ink on our marriage certificate is dry,' he said.

Gabby took another gulping swallow of her drink to disguise her discomfiture. Her stomach felt quivery all of a sudden. The thought of his hands and mouth on her body was making her feel as if she had taken on much more than she had bargained for. She had held Tristan off for years— except for that one horrible night when he had… She swallowed another mouthful of her drink, determined not to think of the degradation she had suffered at her late husband's hands.

'You have gone rather pale,' Vinn observed. 'Is the thought of sharing my bed distasteful to you?'

Gabby was glad she had her glass to hide behind, although the amount of alcohol she had consumed *had* gone alarmingly to her head. Or perhaps it was his disturbing presence. Either way, she didn't trust herself to speak and instead sent him another haughty glare.

'That kiss we shared seven years ago certainly didn't suggest you would find my lovemaking abhorrent—anything but. You were hungry for it, Gabriella. I found that rather interesting, since the following day you married another man.'

'You *forced* yourself on me,' she hissed at him in an undertone, on account of the other diners close by.

'Forced is perhaps too strong a word to use, but in any case you responded wholeheartedly,' he said. 'Not just with those soft full lips of yours, but with your tongue as well. And if I recall even your teeth got into the act at one point. I'm getting hard now, just thinking about it.'

Gabby had never felt so embarrassed in her entire life. Her face felt as if someone had aimed a blowtorch at her. But even more disturbing was the thought of his body stirring with arousal *for her*—especially with those powerful thighs of his within touching distance of hers.

'Your recollection has obviously been distorted over time, for I can barely remember it,' she said with a toss of her head.

His eyes glinted smoulderingly. 'Then perhaps I should refresh your memory,' he said. 'No doubt there will be numerous opportunities to do so once we are living together as man and wife.'

Gabby had to fight to remain calm, but it was almost impossible to control the stuttering of her heart and the flutter of panic deep and low in her belly. 'When do you plan for this ridiculous farce to commence?' she asked, with fabricated quiescence.

'Our marriage will not be a farce,' he said, with a determined set to his mouth. 'It will be real in every sense of the word.'

Her eyes widened a fraction before she could counter it. 'Is that some sort of sick habit of yours? Sleeping with someone you dislike?'

'You are a very beautiful woman, Gabriella,' he said. 'Whether I like you or not is beside the point.'

Gabby wanted to slap that supercilious smile off his face. She sat with her hands clenched in her lap, her eyes shooting sparks of fury at him. But more disturbing was the way her body was responding to his smoothly delivered sensual promises. She could feel a faint trembling between her thighs, like a tiny pulse, and her breasts felt full and tight, her nipples suddenly sensitive against the black fabric of her dress.

'I'm prepared to marry you, but that's as far as it goes,' she said with a testy look. 'It's totally barbaric of you to expect me to agree to a physical relationship with you.'

'Aren't you forgetting something?' he asked. 'Two point four million dollars is a high price for a bride, and I expect to get my money's worth.'

She sucked in a rasping breath. 'This is outrageous! It's akin to prostitution.'

'You came to me for help, Gabriella, and I gave it to you,' he said. 'I was totally up-front about the terms, so there is no point in pretending to be shocked about them now.'

'But what about the woman you were seeing a month or so ago?' Gabby asked, recalling a photograph she had seen in the 'Who's-Out-and-About?' section of one of the Sydney papers. An exquisitely beautiful woman gazing up at Vinn adoringly.

He gave her a supercilious smile. 'So you have been keeping a close eye on my love life, have you, *mia piccola?*'

She glowered at him darkly. 'I have absolutely no interest in who you see. But if we are to suffer a short-term marriage, the very least you could do is keep your affairs out of the press.'

'I don't recall saying our marriage was going to be a short-term one,' he said with an inscrutable smile. 'Far from it.'

Gabby felt her heart give a kick-like movement against the wall of her chest. 'W-what?' she gasped.

'I have always held the opinion that marriage should be for life,' he said. 'I guess you could say it stems from my background. My mother was abandoned by the man she loved while she had a baby on the way. She had no security, no husband to provide for her, and as a result she went on to live a hard life of drudgery—cleaning other people's houses to keep food on the table and clothes on our backs. I swore from an early age that when it came time for me to settle down I would do so with permanence in mind.'

'But you don't even *like* me!' she blurted in shock. 'How could you possibly contemplate tying yourself to me for the rest of your life?'

'Haven't you got any mirrors at your house any more, *mia splendida ragazza?*' he asked, with another smouldering look. 'I do not have to like you to lust over you. And isn't that what every wife wants? A husband with an un-quenchable desire for her and her alone?'

Gabby swallowed back her panic, but even so she felt as if she was choking on a thick uneven lump of it. 'You're winding me up. I know you are. This is your idea of a sick joke. And let me tell you, I am not finding it the least bit amusing.'

'I am not joking, Gabriella,' he said. 'Love is generally an overrated emotion—or at least I have found it to be so. People fall in and out of love all the time. But some of the most success-ful marriages I know are those built on com-patibility in bed—and, believe you me, you don't need to be in love with someone to have an earth-shattering orgasm with them.'

Gabby felt her face explode with colour, and was never more grateful for the reappearance of the waiter to take their meal orders.

Hearing Vinn speak of…that word…*that ex-perience*…made her go hot all over. She had never experienced pleasure with her late husband. The one time Tristan had taken it upon himself to assert "his manly duty", as he had eu-phemistically called it, he had left her not cold, but burning with pain and shame.

Once the waiter had left, Gabby drained the rest of her cocktail, beyond caring that it had made her head spin. No amount of alcohol could affect her more than Vinn had already done, she decided. Her body was tingling all over with sen-sation, and her mind was running off at wayward tangents, imagining what it would feel like to be crushed by the solid weight of his body, his sensual mouth locked on hers, one of his strong, hair-roughened thighs nudging hers apart to—

She jerked away from her thoughts, annoyed that she had allowed his potent brand of sensu-ality to get under her guard. What on earth was she thinking? He was the enemy. She knew exactly what he was doing and why. He was only marrying her to get back at her for how she had treated him in the past. He knew it would be torture for her to be tied to him. Why else would he insist on it? Never had she regretted her immature behaviour more than this moment. Why, oh why, had she been so shallow and cruel?

Gabby's older brother Blair had often pulled her up for her attitude towards Vinn, but in a way his relationship with Vinn had been a huge part of the problem. She had felt *jealous* that her adored older brother clearly preferred the company of the cleaner's son to hers. Gabby had resented the way Blair spent hours helping Vinn with his studies when he could have been spending time with her, the way he'd used to do before Vinn had arrived with his mother.

When Gabby had accidentally stumbled upon the realisation that Vinn suffered from dyslexia she had cruelly taunted him with it, mocking him for not being able to read the most basic of texts. But for some reason, just as he had when she had led him on so despicably that hot summer afternoon when she was sixteen, Vinn had never spoken to her brother or her parents about her behaviour. He had taken it on the chin, removing himself from her presence without a word, even though she had sensed the blistering anger in him, simmering just below the surface of his steely outward calm.

Gabby could sense that anger still simmering now, in the way he looked at her from beneath that slightly hooded brow. Those grey-blue eyes were like mysteriously deep mountain lakes, icy cold one minute, warm and inviting the next, and they spoke of a man who had nothing but revenge on his mind.

She had seen the way women were looking at him. He had such arrestingly handsome features, and his presence was both commanding and brooding—as if he was calculating his next move, like a champion chess player, prepared to take as long as he needed to move his king, making his opponent sit it out in gut-wrenching apprehension.

Gabby felt another shiver of unease pass through her at the thought of being married to him. He had said he expected their marriage to be permanent. That meant there were issues to consider: children, for one thing. She was twenty-eight years old, and she would be lying if she said she hadn't heard the relentless ticking of her biological clock in the two years since Tristan had died. Children had not been an option while she had been married to him. She would *never* have brought children into such a relationship. She hadn't even brought a pet into the house in case he had used it against her in one of his violent moods.

'You have gone very quiet, Gabriella,' Vinn observed. 'Is the thought of having an orgasm with me too hard for you to handle?'

She gave him a withering look. 'No, in actual fact I find it hard to believe it possible,' she said. 'I can't speak for the legion of women you've already bedded, but I personally am unable to engage in such an intimate act without some engagement of emotion.'

He gave a deep chuckle of laughter. 'How about hate?' he asked, reaching for his mineral water. 'Is that enough emotion to get you rolling?'

She put down her glass and signalled for the waiter to refill it.

'Do you think that is wise?' Vinn asked. 'The amount of alcohol in that drink is enough to cloud anyone's judgement.'

Gabby put up her chin. 'In the absence of the engagement of emotion, alcohol and a great deal of it is the next best thing,' she said.

His eyes narrowed to grey-blue stormy slits. 'If you think I will bed you while you are under the influence, think again,' he said. 'When we come together for the first time I want you stone-cold sober, so you remember every second of it.'

Gabby put her glass down with a sharp little clunk. 'I am *not* going to sleep with you, Vinn,' she said, and hoisting up her chin even higher, added imperiously, 'For *that* privilege you will have to pay double.'

Vinn smiled a victor's smile as he reached inside his jacket for his chequebook. He laid it on the table between them, and the click of his pen made Gabby's spine jerk upright, as if she had been shot with a pellet from the gold-embossed barrel.

'Double, you said?'

Gabby felt her stomach drop. Her mouth went dry and her palms moistened. 'Um…I…I'm not sure. I…this…it…I…don't…*Oh, my God…*'

He wrote the amount in his distinctive scrawl, the dark slash of his signature making Gabby's eyes almost pop out of their sockets. 'There,' he said, tearing off the cheque from the book and placing it in front of her on the table. 'Do we have a deal or not?'

CHAPTER THREE

GABBY looked at the amount written there and felt a shockwave of so many emotions rocketing through her that she felt her face fire up. Each one of them stoked the furnace, although shame had by far the most fuel. But then anger joined in; she could feel it blazing out of control, and not just on her cheeks, but deep inside, where a cauldron of heat was bubbling over, making her veins hot with rage.

Vinn had deliberately made her feel like a high-end prostitute—a woman who would do anything for a price. But Gabby wasn't going to be bought. She had been a fool before where a man was concerned, allowing duty and blinkered emotions to cloud her judgement. This time things would be different. If Vinn Venadicci thought he could lure her between the sheets of his bed with a bank vault full of dollar bills, he was in for a big surprise.

With a coolness she was nowhere near feeling, Gabby picked up the cheque and, with the tip of her tongue peeping through her lips as she concentrated, she folded it, fold by meticulous fold, until she had made a tiny origami ship. She held it in the palm of her hand for a moment as she inspected it, and once she was satisfied she had Vinn's full attention she reached for the glass of full-bodied red wine the waiter had recently set down beside him. She dropped her handiwork in, watching in satisfaction as it floated for a second or two, until the density of the wine gradually soaked through the paper and submerged it halfway below the surface.

Gabby met Vinn's grey-blue gaze across the table with an arch look. 'I was going to say you could put your cheque in your pipe and smoke it, but then I realised you don't smoke.' She smiled a cat's smile and added, *'Salute.'*

Vinn's lips twitched, but even so his eyes still burned with determination. 'You might like me to swallow my offer, but I can guarantee you are going to be the one eating your words in the not so distant future, *cara*,' he warned her silkily.

She rolled her eyes and picked up her second cocktail. 'I will go as far as marrying you to save my family's business, but I am not going to be your sex slave, Vinn. If you have the urge to satisfy your needs I am sure there are plenty of women out there who will gladly oblige. All I ask is for you to be discreet.'

He leaned back in his chair and surveyed her features for a beat or two. 'Is that the arrangement you made with your late husband?' he asked. 'Or did you see to his needs quite willingly all by yourself?'

Gabby felt her heart come to a shuddering standstill, her face heating to boiling point. 'That is none of your business,' she bit out. 'I refuse to discuss my marriage to Tristan with you, of all people.'

Vinn's top lip curled in an insolent manner.

'Did he satisfy you, Gabriella? Did he make you writhe and scream? Or did he satisfy you in other ways by lavishing you with the worldly goods women like you crave?'

Gabby's hand tightened around her cocktail glass as she fought to control the bewildering combination of shame and anger that roiled through her. She hadn't thought it possible to hate someone as much as she hated Vinn. She didn't want to examine too closely why she hated him so much, but she suspected it had something to do with the way he looked at her in that penetrating way of his. Those intelligent eyes saw things she didn't want anyone to see. He had done it all those years ago, and he was doing it now.

She forced her tense shoulders to relax and, loosening her white-knuckled grip on her glass, brought it to her mouth and took a sip. 'What about *your* love-life, Vinn?' she asked, with a pert set to her mouth. 'Who's your latest squeeze? Are you still seeing that chainstore model or has she reached her use-by date?'

Vinn used his fork to retrieve the sunken boat of his cheque out of his glass before he trained his gaze on hers. 'Have you been taking extra classes in bitchiness, Gabriella, or is it that time of the month?'

Gabby knew she shouldn't do it, but even as the mature and sensible part of her brain considered the repercussions, the outraged part had already acted.

It seemed to happen in slow motion. The strawberry daiquiri in her glass moved in a fluid arc and splashed across the front of Vinn's shirt.

Time didn't just stand still; it came to a screeching, rubber burning, tyre-balding halt.

Gabby waited for the fall-out. Her body grew tense, her blood raced, her heart thumped. But in the end all Vinn did was laugh.

'Is that the best you can do, Gabriella?' he asked, still smiling mockingly. 'To toss your drink across the table like a recalcitrant three-year-old child?'

'If you are expecting me to apologise, then

forget it. Because I'm not going to,' she said with a petulant glare.

He put the soiled napkin to one side. 'No,' he said, still smiling in that enigmatic way of his that unnerved her so. 'I wasn't expecting you to apologise now. I am looking forward to making you do so later, when we are not sitting in the middle of a crowded restaurant. And believe me, Gabriella, it will be a lot of fun making you do it.'

Gabby felt a moth-like flutter of apprehension sweep over the floor of her belly. She had faced numerous rages from Tristan in the past, but for some reason Vinn's cool, calm control was far more terrifying. But then Vinn had always been cool and controlled. Even when she had taunted him in the past he had taken it on the chin, looking down at her with those unreadable grey-blue eyes. Perhaps that was why he had become so successful over the years? He knew how to play people like some people played cards, and Gabby had a feeling he had just put down a hand that was going to be impossible for her to beat.

'Is everything all right, Signor Venadicci?' The *maître d'* came bustling over.

'Everything is perfectly all right, thank you, Paolo,' Vinn said with an urbane smile. 'My fiancée had a slight accident.'

'Oh, dear,' Paolo said, and quickly tried to make amends. 'Let me get the young lady another drink—on the house, of course. And send me the bill for the cleaning of your shirt. I am sure the table is rickety, or something. I have asked my staff to check, but you know how hard it is to keep track of everyone all the time.'

'It is fine—really,' Vinn said, rising to his feet. 'We are leaving in any case.'

Gabby was half in and half out of her chair, not sure what she should do. They hadn't even been served their meals and she was starving. She had missed lunch, and already she could feel a headache pounding at the backs of her eyes.

'Leaving?' Paolo said, looking aghast. 'But what about your food?'

'I am sorry, Paolo,' Vinn said. 'Could we have

our meals packaged to take back to my house instead? My fiancée has had rather a tough day, and I think she needs an early night.'

'But of course, Signor Venadicci,' Paolo said, and quickly signalled to his waiting staff to see to it straight away. 'Congratulations on your engagement,' he added, smiling widely at Gabby. 'Such wonderful news. You are a very lucky woman. Signor Venadicci is…how you say in English? A big catch?'

'Yes,' Gabby said with saccharine-sweetness. 'He is a big catch. Just like a shark.'

Vinn grasped her by the arm and practically frogmarched her out of the restaurant, only stopping long enough at the front counter to collect their take-out meals.

'You can let go of my arm now,' she said, once they were on the street outside.

Vinn kept pulling her along towards his car, not even bothering to shorten his much longer stride to accommodate hers. 'You, young lady, need a lesson in manners. You have acted like a spoilt child. You didn't just embarrass yourself, but each and every person in that restaurant—not to mention Paolo, who always bends over backwards to please his diners. You should be ashamed of yourself.'

Gabby gave him a surly look as she tugged ineffectually at his hold. 'You started it.'

He aimed a remote control at his car. 'I asked you a question about your last marriage,' he said, opening the door for her. 'A yes or no answer would have done.'

She sent him a venomous glare. 'I don't have to answer any of your stupid questions, about my marriage or any of my relationships,' she threw at him.

'I can tell you one thing, Gabriella,' he said as he wrenched the seatbelt down for her with a savagery that was unnerving. 'Once we are married you will have no other relationships. Or at least none with a male.'

Gabby sat stiffly in her seat, trying to control her sudden and totally unexpected urge to cry.

She had become very good at concealing her emotions. She had never given Tristan the satisfaction of seeing her break emotionally. Why she should feel so close to the edge now was not only bewildering but terrifying.

She couldn't allow Vinn to see how undone she was. He would relish in the power he had over her. He already had too much power over her— far more than Tristan Glendenning had ever had, in spite of all she had suffered at his hands. How could she afford to let her guard down even for a second? Especially given how she had treated Vinn in the past? Vinn had every reason to bring her down, to make her grovel, to grind what was left of her pride to dust. She had just enough self-respect to keep that from happening.

Not much…but just enough.

Vinn drove his powerful car across the Harbour Bridge to the North Shore suburb of Mosman. Each thrusting gear-change he executed set Gabby's teeth on edge, and another icy shiver of unease scuttled up her spine at the thought of a showdown with him on his own territory. In the crowded restaurant it had been safe to spar with him, or so she had thought. But being alone with him was something she wasn't quite prepared for and wondered if she ever would be.

He turned the car into a beautiful tree-lined street of the sort of homes owned by people with more than just comfortable wealth. Lush gardens, harbour views and stately mansions, with the mandatory fortress-like security that ensured a private haven away from the rest of the world. They indicated Vinn had made his way in the world and wasn't ashamed about taking his place in it amongst others who had done similarly—either by sheer hard work or the inheritance of a family fortune.

The driveway he turned into after activating a remote control device revealed a modern caramel-coloured mansion with a three-tiered formal garden at the front. Gabby could see the high fence of a tennis court in the background, and heard the sound of a trickling fountain close by. The heady scent of purple wisteria was heavy in the air, and so too was the more subtle fragrance of night-scented stocks, growing in profusion in a bed that ran alongside the boundary of the property.

She breathed in the clove-like smell, wondering if Vinn had somehow remembered they were one of her favourite flowers. She loved the variety of colours, the way the thick stalks didn't always stand up straight, and how the individual clusters of blossom maintained their scent right to the last. And yet perversely, if housed in a vase indoors, the water they sat in became almost fetid, as if those stately and proud blooms resented being confined.

Vinn unlocked the front door and indicated for her to precede him, which Gabby did with an all-encompassing sweep of her gaze. The marbled foyer was not in the least as ostentatious as she had been expecting. Even the works of art on the walls spoke of individual taste rather than an attempt to belong to a particularly highbrow club of art appreciation.

One painting in particular drew her eye: it was of a small child, a boy, looking at a shell on the seashore, his tiny limbs in a crouched position, his gaze focussed on the shell in his hands as if it contained all the mysteries of the world. Gabby peered at the right-hand corner of the canvas but she couldn't make out the signature.

'You don't recognise the artist?' Vinn said from just behind her left shoulder.

Gabby shivered at his closeness, but, schooling her features, faced him impassively, taking a careful step backwards to create some distance. 'No,' she said. 'Should I?'

His gaze was trained on the canvas, his mouth set in a grim line. 'Probably not,' he said. 'He was always a little embarrassed about his desire to paint. This is the only one I managed to convince him not to destroy.' He paused for a moment before adding, 'I believe it is one of the last works he did before he died.'

'Oh…' Gabby said renewing her focus on the painting. 'Was he very old?'

'No,' Vinn said. 'But then he wasn't the first and I dare say won't be the last artist to succumb to deep-seated insecurities about his talent. It more or less comes with the territory. Being creative can be both a blessing and a burden, or so I have heard people say.'

'Yes…I suppose so…'Gabby answered, still looking at the painting, which for some inexplicable reason had moved her so much.

Perhaps it was because looking at that small innocent child made her think longingly of having her own precious baby one day, she thought. Unlike most of her peers, she had never been interested in pursuing a demanding career. For years all she had dreamed of was holding a baby of her own in her arms, watching him or her grow into teenage, and then adulthood, just as her parents had done with her and Blair.

'We have some things to discuss,' Vinn said, and gestured for her to follow him to the large lounge room off the wide hall.

Gabby took an uneven breath and followed

him into a stylishly appointed room. Two large black leather sofas sat either side of a fireplace— the shiny black marble mantelpiece and surround in a smaller room would have been too much, but not in this room. An ankle-deep rug in a black and gold design softened the masculine feel, as did the vintage lamps sitting on the art deco side tables. A large ottoman doubled as a coffee table, and a state-of-the-art music and entertainment system was cleverly concealed behind a drop-down console.

'It's a nice room,' Gabby said as she perched on the edge of one of the sofas. 'In fact the whole house is lovely. Have you lived here long?'

Vinn leaned his hip against the armrest of the opposite sofa. 'Well, what do you know?' he drawled. 'A compliment from the high and mighty Gabriella St Clair.'

Gabby screwed up her mouth at him. 'Glendenning,' she corrected him, even though she loathed her married name for all it had represented. 'My surname is still Glendenning.'

Something gleamed in Vinn's eyes as they collided with hers. 'But not for much longer,' he said. 'I have already seen to the notice. Shortly we will be husband and wife and living here as such.'

Gabby got to her feet in an agitated manner. 'I don't see what the rush is for,' she said, pacing the floor. 'What are people going to think?'

'For god's sake, Gabriella,' he said, with a flash of impatience in his tone. 'You've been a widow for two years.'

She turned around to look at him. 'Yes…but to suddenly be with you seems…well, it seems…almost indecent,' she said. 'People will think it's a shotgun marriage or something.'

He came over to where she was standing with her arms folded tightly across her chest. She considered moving sideways, but as if he knew she was looking for an escape route he placed both of his hands either side of her head on the wall behind, effectively trapping her.

Gabby felt her eyes flare with panic. She wasn't used to being so close to him. This close, she could smell the tangy lemon of his after-shave. She could even see the regrowth of stubble on his jaw, making her fingers twitch to reach up and feel if it was as raspy and masculine as it looked. She could see the deep-water-blue of his eyes with their grey shadows locked on hers. The line of his mouth was firm, but soft at the same time, making her wonder if his kiss would be just as enthralling as it had been seven years ago.

'You know, Gabriella,' he said in a low velvet tone, 'we could do something about that right here and now.'

Gabby's throat tightened as his body brushed against hers. She felt the stirring of his erection, a heady reminder of all that was different between them. He was so experienced, while she was…well, perhaps not exactly inexperienced, but way out of his class. Her body was not tutored in giving and receiving pleasure. She was totally inadequate, lacking in both confidence and skill.

Gabby was in no doubt of Vinn's attraction for her. If she was honest with herself she had been aware of it for years. It was like an electric current that throbbed in the air every time they were in the same room together. She wasn't sure if other people were aware of it, although Tristan had commented on it in his scathing way more than once.

Gabby knew it was just a physical thing on Vinn's part. Men were like that. Especially men like Vinn, who were used to having any woman who took their fancy. He was only attracted to Gabby because for so many years she had been unattainable. She was the daughter of a rich man, while he was the bastard son of a strapped-for-cash house-cleaner. The only trouble was he was prepared to go to unbelievable lengths to have her, even after all this time.

And that he was determined to have her in every sense of the word was as clear as the jagged scar that interrupted the dark slash of his left eyebrow. Apparently he had received it in a drunken brawl the night before her wedding to

Tristan. Though it had only been after she'd come back from their honeymoon that Gabby's mother had told her how Vinn had spent a night in hospital after becoming involved in a punch-up. Given their heated exchange that night, Gabby suspected he had gone out to get himself trashed and had ended up in a street brawl—as he had done several times during his early twenties.

'So what do you say, Gabriella?' Vinn said, one of his strong thighs nudging between hers suggestively, temptingly, and oh, so spine-tinglingly. 'We could make a baby right here and now, and then it would indeed be a shotgun marriage.'

Gabby's stomach hollowed. Her legs felt like waterlogged noodles—too soggy to keep her upright. Her heart was racing, but not with any sort of predictable rhythm. Every second beat or so felt as if it was just off the mark, making her feel light-headed. Her unruly mind was suddenly filled with images—disturbing, toe-curling images—of his body pumping with purpose into the tight cocoon of hers, nudging her womb, filling it with his life force, his cells meshing with hers to create a new life.

Somehow she managed to activate her voice, but it sounded as if it had come from somewhere deep inside her, croaky, rusty and disjointed. 'I—I'm not interested in…having a child,' she said. 'Not with you.'

'I am not going to settle for a childless marriage,' he said. 'I have paid a high price for you, Gabriella. As part of that heavy financial commitment I expect a return on my investment.'

Gabby shoved him away, both of her hands flat on his rock-hard chest. 'Then you've bought the wrong bride,' she flashed at him angrily. 'It's bad enough that you want this arrangement to be permanent, but to want children as well is nothing short of ludicrous.'

'I never said anything to suggest this wasn't going to be a proper marriage,' he said. 'Two point four million dollars is not pin money, Gabriella. A divorce could turn out to be even more expensive—although I have that covered with my legal advisors. Tomorrow you will sign a prenuptial agreement that will ensure the only benefit you will receive if our marriage does for some reason fail will be an income to pay for your manicures and the highlights in your hair.'

Gabby was almost beyond rage. Her whole body felt as if it was going to explode with it. She wanted to pummel him with her fists; she wanted to scratch at his face, to make him feel some small measure of the pain she was feeling.

Vinn made her feel like a shallow socialite who had nothing better to do with her time that have her nails filed and her hair bleached. But she was so much more than that. She hadn't been before, but after the death of her brother—not to mention the five years of her marriage to Tristan Glendenning, had taught her how shallow her life had been and how much she had wanted it to change.

And she *had* changed.

She had changed in so many ways. Not all of them were visible, but they were changes she was still working on daily. Taking up the reins of her father's company was something she hadn't really had much choice over, but she wasn't a quitter and would see it through—as Blair surely would have done if his personal issues hadn't got in the way.

Thinking about her brother always stirred the long-handled spoon of guilt in her stomach, its churning action making her feel sick with anguish. If only she had known about his drug use she might have been able to help him before it was too late. But he had preferred to face death than his family's disappointment, and she would always blame herself for her part in that.

She resumed her seat on the cloud-soft sofa, her trembling hands stuffed between her equally unsteady thighs, fighting not to show how close to breaking she was. No doubt Vinn would relish that. He would be silently gloating over finally breaking her spirit.

She was trapped.

The steel bars of her guilt had closed around her with a clanging, chilling finality. Vinn had all the power now, and would wield it as he saw fit. He had insisted on marriage—but not the sort of hands-off arrangement she had naively thought he'd had in mind. She had no hope of repaying the money he had put up to save her father's business. It would take her two lifetimes to scrape together even half of that amount. Vinn had known that from the very first moment she had stepped into his office. He had played her like a master, reeling her in, keeping his cards close to his chest as was his custom, revealing them only when it was too late for her to do anything to get out of the arrangement.

It *was* too late.

She was going to be Vinn Venadicci's wife; the only trouble was he had no idea what sort of bride he had just bought. He had paid a huge price, but she was going to be a disappointment.

Of that she was heart-wrenchingly sure.

CHAPTER FOUR

VINN was still leaning on the edge of the sofa, silently watching the myriad moods pass over Gabriella's face. He was well used to seeing anger, rebellion and petulance there; even the bright sheen of moisture in her toffee-brown eyes was something he was used to witnessing. But whether or not those tears were genuine was something he wasn't prepared to lay a bet on.

She was a devious little madam. He had suffered at her hands too many times to let his guard down now. He wasn't going to give an inch until the papers were signed and she was legally his wife—in name if not yet in body.

He could wait.

He had waited for seven years. He figured

waiting a little longer would only increase the pleasure of finally possessing her.

As soon as he had set eyes on her all those years ago he had been struck almost dumb by how beautiful she was. He had watched her blossom from an uncertain and overweight girl of fourteen into a young woman on the threshold of full adulthood. She had grown into an exquisitely beautiful young woman by the time she was sixteen years old, with those wide Bambi eyes and her lusciously thick blonde hair a striking contrast to her darker eyebrows and sooty black lashes. Her full lips were cherry-red, and plump and soft with sensual promise. By the time she was seventeen her teasing smile and come-hither looks had tortured him by day and kept him writhing in frustration in bed at night with the thought of one day possessing her. But even though his body had throbbed with longing he had known it would take nothing short of a miracle to bring about her capitulation.

Gabriella St Clair was out of his league. Vinn had known it, although he had never really accepted it.

Blair St Clair had in his quiet, polite way gently hinted at it, and Gabriella's parents—particularly her mother, Pamela—had communicated it without pulling any punches. It had been made perfectly clear to Vinn that Gabriella's future lay with Tristan Glendenning, an up-and-coming lawyer from a long line of legal eagles, primed to be a partner in a big city firm once he settled down to marriage to his mother's best friend's daughter.

The thing that sickened Vinn the most was that he had never believed Gabriella had truly been in love with her husband—which in itself showed how shallow she was. She couldn't have been in love with Glendenning after the way she had responded to Vinn outside the bathroom the night before her wedding.

She had clung to him feverishly, her soft lips opening to the pressure of his, her tongue darting into his mouth, tasting him, teasing him, duelling with him in a totally carnal explosion of passion that had left them both panting and breathless.

Vinn's hands had uncovered her breasts and shaped them worshipfully, relishing in the creamy softness of them, and she had done nothing to stop him, rather had whimpered and gasped in delight with each touch of his hands, lips and tongue.

Her hands had reached down and cupped the aching bulk of his manhood, stroking him, torturing him until he'd been fit to burst. He would have thrust her up against the nearest wall and driven into her right then and there if it hadn't been for the sound of a footfall on the staircase, and Tristan Glendenning's private academy-tutored voice calling out.

'Gabs? Are you up here? I have to get going. Sorry, babe, but I have a few things to see to before the ceremony tomorrow.'

Vinn had put Gabriella from him almost roughly, raking a hand through his hair in the hope that it would restore some sort of order to it after her fingers had clawed at him in fervent response. Although his breathing was ragged, his heart hammering and his body aching with the pressure of release denied, he had somehow held himself together—but it had taken a monumental effort on his part.

Gabriella, consummate liar and actress that she was, had simply turned with a covert straightening of her clothing and smiled sweetly at her unsuspecting fiancé, with not a single sign of what had transpired just moments ago showing anywhere on her person. Her brown eyes had been clear and steady on his, her voice smooth and even.

'You're leaving already?' she'd asked, with just the right amount of disappointment in her tone. 'But you only just got here. You missed the rehearsal and everything.'

Tristan had leaned in and lightly kissed her swollen mouth. 'I know, dearest, but I'll make it up to you on our honeymoon, I promise. Besides, it's almost midnight. Isn't it bad luck or something to see the bride before she gets to the church?'

Vinn had pushed past them, his gut churning, his

fists clenched so tight he'd thought each and every one of the bones in his hands would surely crack.

'Are you off now too, Venadicci?' Tristan had asked in a condescending tone. 'No doubt you have plenty to do, helping your mother polish the silver, hey what?'

Vinn had forced his mouth into a stiff movement of his lips that was nowhere close to a smile. 'You would be amazed at how tarnished some of those St Clair silver spoons are,' he'd said, and with one last searing glance at Gabriella strode down the hall.

Gabby lifted her head after a long silence and felt her heart give a little flutter of unease when she saw Vinn's penetrating look. 'You're really serious about this, aren't you?' she asked in a voice that came out thready. 'But why, Vinn? You're a rich man now. You've made it in the world. Why insist on marrying me?'

He pushed himself away from the sofa and came and stood right in front of her, so she had to crane her neck to look up at him. 'You still don't get it, do you, Gabriella?' he said, his eyes burning into hers. 'I don't want any other woman. Not since that night when I could have taken you up against the wall outside your upstairs bathroom. You wanted it, just as much as I wanted it so don't bother insulting my intelligence by denying it.'

Shame hoisted Gabby to her feet, her eyes blazing in fury. 'That's a despicable lie! You took advantage of me,' she threw at him, knowing it wasn't strictly true but saying it anyway. 'You were always leering at me. You did it every time you visited your mother at the house.'

Vinn's mouth stretched into a sneer. 'That's how you like to recall it, isn't it, Gabriella?' he asked. 'But I seem to remember it a little differently. You liked to flirt and tease, and you used every opportunity you could to do so. You got a perverse sort of pleasure out of dangling before me what I couldn't have, like taunting a starving dog with a juicy bone. Remember all those hot afternoons by the pool, when you knew I was going to be around to mow the lawn or trim the hedges? I knew what you were up to. You wanted me to make a move on you so you could cry wolf to your father and have me and my mother evicted. That was your game, wasn't it? You didn't even want your brother spending time with me. You were jealous he'd started to prefer my company to yours.'

Gabby's face flamed as she recalled how brazen and obvious she had been. Yes, she *had* been jealous of Vinn's friendship with her brother, but it had been about much more than that. From the moment Vinn had arrived at the St Clair mansion Gabby had felt uncomfortable in a way she couldn't adequately describe. She had only just turned fourteen at the time, and certainly Vinn, although being four years older, had never given her any reason to feel under threat. He'd mostly kept to himself, keeping his eyes downcast as he went about the odd jobs Gabby's father had organised for him.

It had only been as she'd grown from a young teen into a young woman that Gabby had begun to notice the way she felt when their eyes chanced to meet. It was unlike anything she had ever felt before with anyone else—even Tristan, who everyone knew would one day be her husband.

Looking into Vinn Venadicci's startlingly attractive grey-blue eyes now was like looking into the centre of a flame. The heat came back at her, scorching her until she had to drop her gaze.

'For God's sake, Vinn, I was what? Fifteen or sixteen?' she said, in what even she realised was a pathetic attempt to belatedly right the wrongs of the past. 'Surely you're not going to hold that against me?'

He gave a coarse-sounding laugh. 'My mother was right about you,' he said, raking her with his gaze. 'She said when the highest bidder came along you would sell your soul, and that's exactly what you did. Tristan Glendenning wanted shares in your father's business, and you were the little blonde bonus thrown in for free.'

Gabby clenched her teeth, her eyes sparking with anger, her whole body shaking with it. 'That's an atrocious and totally insulting thing to say,' she tossed back. 'Tristan's mother was my mother's best friend. They were each other's bridesmaids. It was always expected Tristan and I would marry. We grew up together, and apart from when my brother and Tristan were away at boarding school we spent most of our weekends and holidays together.' She paused for a nano-second before adding, perhaps not as convincingly as she would have liked, 'It's…it was what we both wanted.'

Vinn gave a chillingly ruthless smile. 'Did he get his money's worth, Gabriella?' he asked. 'Were you a dutiful, obedient little wife for him?'

Gabby couldn't bear to look at the unmitigated disgust on his face. It was like confronting every stupid mistake she had ever made. How had she not known what sort of husband Tristan Glendenning would turn out to be? How could she have been so blind? She had no excuse. It wasn't as if Tristan had been a perfect stranger. She had known him all her life. And yet there had been things about him she had not known until it was too late.

Gabby spun away from Vinn's harsh expression. But the too sudden movement made her stomach heave, and her face and hands became clammy as she struggled to stay upright. She reached for the nearest arm of the sofa but her hand couldn't quite connect: it flailed in mid-air, like a ghost's hand passing through solid substance, and she felt herself go down in slow motion. Her knees buckled first and then her legs folded. Her head was spinning, and her eyes were unable to stay open as the room swirled sickeningly before her…

'Gabriella?' Vinn was on his knees, cradling her head in his hands before it connected with the floor.

She made a soft sound—more like a groan than anything else. But at least it meant she was still conscious. She was like a lifeless doll—a beautiful porcelain doll with the stuffing knocked out of it. At first he wondered if she was acting. It had all seemed so staged. And yet when he placed his hand on her smooth brow it was clammy. It made him wonder if he had mis-judged her. Yes, things had been stressful lately for her—the margin call and her father's illness would have knocked anyone sideways—but the Gabriella he knew from the past would have played her histrionics to the hilt. A timely swoon or faint was well within her repertoire.

'Are you all right?' he asked, frowning in spite of his lingering doubts.

'W-what happened?' she said, opening her eyes, wincing against the light.

'You fainted, apparently,' Vinn said, although he still cradled her in his arms. She was lighter than he remembered, soft and feminine, and her scent was so alluring he couldn't stop his nostrils from flaring to breathe more of her in.

She groaned again and turned her head away. 'I think I'm going to be sick…'

Vinn decided he had better not take any risks,

and quickly scooped her up and took her to the closest bathroom, holding her gently as she leaned over the basin. He winced in empathy as she emptied her stomach, her slim body shuddering with each racking heave.

'Are you done?' he asked, after a moment or two of keeping her steady.

Her hands gripped the edge of the basin, her head still bent low. 'Please…leave me alone for a minute…' she said hoarsely. 'I'm not used to having an audience at times…like this.'

'I'm not leaving you until I am certain you aren't going to knock yourself out cold on the edge of the basin or on the tiled floor,' he said. 'You scared the hell out of me.'

Vinn noticed her hands tighten their hold on the basin, making her small knuckles go white. She swayed slightly again, her eyes closing against another wave of nausea. He quickly rinsed a facecloth and, lifting the curtain of her hair, dabbed it at the back of her neck, just as his mother had done whenever he was sick as a child.

Gabby finally pushed herself back from the basin. Taking the facecloth from him, she buried her face in it, conscious of Vinn's firm but gentle hand in the small of her back, moving in a circular and bone-meltingly soothing motion.

'No more cocktails for you, young lady,' he said. 'They obviously don't agree with you.'

Gabby pressed her fingers to her temples. 'Maybe you're right,' she said, turning to face him, her body suddenly feeling weak and unsupported without the touch of his warm hand on her back. 'Would you mind if I go home now? It's kind of been a long day…' She gave a jaded sigh. 'Actually, it's been a long week…'

His eyes meshed with hers for an infinitesimal moment.

'Gabriella,' he said, 'your father is going to make it. People have triple heart bypass surgery all the time, and most if not all go on to make a full recovery.'

She bit her bottom lip and lowered her eyes from his. 'I know… It's just that he's depending on me. I don't want to let him down. I can't let him know about…about…' she flapped one of her hands '…about this margin call.'

He put his hands on the tops of her shoulders. 'The resort is secure,' he said, giving her shoulders a gentle squeeze. 'After we are married I want us to go there and check out the redevelopment. People will expect us to go on a honeymoon, so it will be a perfect excuse to do both.'

He felt her tense under his hands. 'I don't want to be too far away from my parents just now,' she said, not quite holding his gaze.

'Gabriella, you have to live your own life,' he said. 'It is your mother's responsibility to support your father, not yours. You have done enough. To be quite frank, I think you've done too much.'

A glitteringly defiant light came into her eyes as they warred with his. 'I don't want to go on a honeymoon with you, Vinn,' she said. 'Do I have to spell it out any plainer than that? I'm not going to sleep with you.'

Vinn let out his breath on a long-winded stream

in an effort to contain his patience, which was already fraying at the edges. 'You know something?' he said. 'As much as I would like to, I am not going to throw you onto the nearest surface and ravish you, Gabriella. I understand you will need time to adjust to our marriage. I am prepared to give you the time you need, within reason.'

She tossed her head at him. 'Oh, yes?' she said with a scathing look. 'Within reason. Whatever that might mean. What…a couple of days? A week or two? A month?'

His eyes lasered hers. 'I told you, I want our marriage to be a real one.'

She began to push past him towards the door with an embittered scowl. 'Do you even *know* what a real marriage is about? You were the child of a single mother. You have no idea how a marriage works.'

'You were married for five years,' he inserted coolly as he put his hand on the bathroom door, closing it firmly to stop her escaping. 'How about you tell *me*?'

Gabby felt as if he had kicked her in the tenderest part of her belly, where all her hurt, all her disappointment and all her guilt were contained in one gnarled mass of miserable agony. She had to fight not to double over with the pain of it. It was crippling, agonising to withstand it, but only her strength of will kept her upright.

She would *not* break in front of him.

Vengeance was his goal, but she was not going to give in to him—and certainly not with her pride as a garnish. That was what he was after. He wanted her to grovel and beg and wear a hair shirt for the rest of her life. But she was not going to allow him to humble her.

She wasn't going to do it. Not without a fight.

She stood in place, like a fountain that had suddenly been frozen. Even the bitter tears at the backs of her eyes had turned to dry ice, burning but not flowing.

'I can tell you, Vinn, that marriage takes a whole lot more work than a few fancy-sounding promises muttered in front of a minister of religion,' she said. 'What you are asking for is a commitment that no one can really guarantee, and certainly not without love. It seems to me the only motivation you have for this union of ours is vengeance.'

Vinn's top lip lifted. 'You're surely not expecting me to *love* you, Gabriella?' he asked.

Gabby briefly closed her eyes in pain, but when she opened them again she saw the same caustic bitterness glittering in his; it hadn't gone away, and it surprised her how devastated she felt to realise it was never likely to. He would always look at her with hate blazing in his eyes and revenge simmering in his blood.

'No,' she said, almost inaudibly, 'I don't expect you to love me.'

Vinn reached past her to turn on the shower head. 'Have a shower while I find something for you to sleep in tonight,' he said. 'There is no way I am going to allow you to spend the night alone at your parents' house. You can stay here with me. There are fresh towels on the heated rail.'

Gabby's hands grasped at the basin again for balance. 'I don't need a shower—and I am not sleeping in this house with—'

He ignored her and thrust a bottle of perfumed body wash into her hands. 'As much as I hate to contradict you, Gabriella,' he said, 'you have not only managed to cover yourself in your own sickness, but me as well. Now, get into that damned shower before I change my mind and get in there with you.'

Gabby threw him a fulminating glare, but she took the body wash from him with hands not quite steady. 'Has anyone ever told you what a bull-headed brute you are?' she said.

He put his hands on his hips and stared her down. 'Get in the shower, Gabriella. You're wasting water.'

Gabby stepped into the huge shower stall, clothes and all, and on an impulse she really couldn't account for lifted off the removable shower head and aimed it straight at him.

Water went everywhere—all over the marbled

walls and tiled floor, but most of all on Vinn's face and upper body, before he could snatch control of it.

'Why, you little wildcat,' he growled and, stepping into the shower with her, gave her a dose of her own watery medicine.

'Stop it!' Gabby squealed as the hot fine needles of water stung her face and shoulders. 'I'm fully dressed, you idiot!'

'So you are,' he said and, hanging the shower head back up, turned off the water. 'But then so am I and these are a brand-new pair of trousers.'

Gabby stood there dripping, caught between the urge to grab back the shower head and douse him all over again, and the even more disturbing urge to pull his glistening head down so his mouth could fuse hotly with hers.

How had the atmosphere changed so rapidly? she wondered dazedly. The air was suddenly thick with sexual attraction, heavy and pulsing, especially in a silence measured through electrically charged second with a series of plops and drips that sounded like rifle-shots.

Gabby brushed a slick strand of hair off her face with a hand that shook slightly. 'I hope you're not expecting me to pay for your trousers, because I'm not going to,' she said—more for something to say to break the dangerously sensual spell.

'No,' he said, looking at her dripping mouth and chin, his own face and hair soaking wet. 'I was thinking more along the lines of you paying a penalty in another currency entirely.'

Gabby licked the droplets of water off her mouth, trying to control the hit-and-miss beat of her heart. 'I'm n-not sure what you mean…' she said, stepping back as far as the shower cubicle would allow. But it wasn't far enough. For that matter Perth, on the other side of the continent, wouldn't be far enough.

She felt the cold hard-marbled wall at her back, and when Vinn stepped closer she felt his wet shirt and trousers come into contact with her sodden black dress. Never had the expensive designer fabric of her outfit seemed so thin, Gabby thought. She could feel Vinn's belt buckle pressing into her belly, and not only his buckle but his growing erection as well. It was rock-hard, and so close to the aching pulse of her body she couldn't breathe.

'What about it, Gabriella?' he asked in a smoulderingly sexy tone. 'What say we strip off and finish this properly? That's the game you want to play, isn't it? It's just like the game you wanted to play in the past. Let's get Vinn all hot under the collar so he acts like a rutting animal, right? That's what you want, isn't it?'

Gabriella was shocked at how much she wanted to rise to his challenging statement. She did want to rip his shirt from his broad chest and press her mouth on each of his flat male nipples in turn. She did want to unfasten his belt and expose his engorged male flesh to the exploration of her fingers, to feel the strength and power of his blood pulsing through him. She wanted to have him press her back against the marbled wall of the shower, his hands cupping and kneading her breasts, his mouth moving moistly over each tight nipple, until every thought flew out of her head.

But that was the trouble. Her head and all the thoughts inside it. The swirling, torturous thoughts that reminded her in that taunting, unrelenting tone how useless she was at seduction. She was a novice at lovemaking. Her own husband had found her body a total turn-off, so disgusting he had sought the company of other women.

'Gabriella?' Vinn tipped up her chin, a frown bringing his brows together. 'Are you cold? I'm sorry—I didn't notice how much you were shivering. Here, let me turn the water back on.'

Gabby was shaking. Not from cold, but from the effort of keeping a lid on her emotions. Never had she felt more outmatched, outmanoeuvred and totally powerless. Vinn had her in the palm of his hand, and if she didn't find an excuse to get him out of the bathroom within the next few seconds she knew she was going to fall apart completely.

Somehow having him witness her at her lowest point was too much to bear right now. How he would gloat and mock her for all she had represented. She could hardly blame him; she had been such a fool, a silly little insecure fool, who hadn't for a moment considered his feelings. He had every right to hate her, to want to avenge all the petty wrongs of the past. That was why he was marrying her—to bring her under his control, to humble her, to gloat over his possession of her.

'N-no, I'm not c-cold,' she said, although she was shivering. 'B-but I would like to be alone.'

Vinn adjusted the water to make it slightly warmer before he stepped out of the cubicle. 'I'll get you something to wear,' he said, and reached for a towel to dry off before he left her.

He came back to stand outside the bathroom door a few minutes later, with a tracksuit which was at least four sizes too big for her. Although the shower was now turned off, he could hear the muffled sound of Gabriella sniffing, as if she had been crying. Something pulled in his chest, like a string tied to his heart, but he staunchly ignored it. Tears and tantrums were some of the many tools in Gabriella's arsenal: she used them interchangeably to get her way. How many times in the past had he been fooled by carefully orchestrated tears? He was no such lovesick fool now—no way. He had wised up and wised up well. Gabriella had a lot riding on maintaining his goodwill right now, and he was going to make the most of it.

When she finally came out, after he had handed her the tracksuit through a crack in the door, there was no sign of distress on her face. Her eyes were clear, and if anything characteristically defiant. And he had to admit, dressed as she was in his clothes, she looked like a small child. She had rolled up the arms and the legs, but with her hair still wet and hanging about her shoulders she looked tiny and fragile and totally adorable.

Vinn felt a momentary tug at his heart again, but just as quickly ignored it. This was not the time to go all soft on her. They had a deal, and he was going to make certain she fulfilled her side of it.

'Maybe I will take you home after all,' he said gruffly. 'As your father's surgery has been rescheduled for tomorrow morning. Let's get past that hurdle before we deal with the next.'

'Thanks, Vinn...' she said, in a whisper-soft voice, her eyes lowering from his. 'This has all been such a terrible shock to me...'

Vinn wanted to ask what she was referring to: his demand for marriage or her father's health scare? But he didn't, because he already knew the answer.

The Gabriella St Clair he knew would take her father's heart attack in her stride. But being forced to marry the bastard son of the St Clair house-cleaner was something else again.

CHAPTER FIVE

GABBY chewed her nails one by one as she'd waited with her mother in the relatives' lounge for news of her father's condition. It had been a long wait, for although Henry St Clair had been first on the list, the procedure usually took anything up to three or four hours, as veins were harvested from the lower legs to relocate in the chest as heart valves.

Finally the surgeon came out with good news. Everything had gone extremely well, and Henry was in recovery. He would be there for quite some time, before being transferred to Intensive Care, and then to the high-dependency unit a few days later.

'When can we see him?' Gabby asked, holding onto her mother's hand and squeezing it tightly.

'As soon as he is transferred to the ICU I will have someone inform you,' the surgeon said. 'Try not to be too put off by all the machines and drips attached to him. It all looks a lot scarier than it really is, I can assure you. He is one of the luckier ones. He hasn't smoked in years, and his weight is within the normal range. A family history of heart disease is, of course, unfortunate, but with the right lifestyle changes he should make a very good recovery, as long as his stress levels are kept down during rehabilitation.'

Gabby couldn't have heard more convincing words. The pre-nuptial agreement papers she had signed first thing that morning sent via express courier had been worth it. She was committed to marrying Vinn Venadicci in front of a marriage celebrant in a registry office. They would be leaving for a short honeymoon at the St Clair Island Resort later the same day.

Gabby tried not to think too much about it all,

and was almost glad she had her father to worry about instead. It gave her a focus, supporting her mother, who didn't cope well even with breaking a nail or her roots showing, let alone a crisis of this sort. Her mother's reaction to Blair's death had been part of the reason Gabby had agreed to marry Tristan Glendenning, even though she had been having doubts for months. Tristan had assured her a big wedding to plan was just the thing to get her mother out of bed each day, and off the strong and highly addictive sedatives the doctor had prescribed.

Gabby's concern over her mother's health and wellbeing had more or less sealed her own fate. She had been so distracted by her parents and their heart-wrenching grief she had more or less had to ignore her own, and in so doing had set in motion years of hell.

Now she was doing it all over again. She was marrying a man she didn't love in order to protect those she loved with all her heart.

But for some reason Gabby didn't feel Vinn

would be in quite the same category of husband as Tristan. Perhaps that was why she was feeling so unsettled. Vinn was a mystery to her. In many ways he always had been. That was what she found so intriguing about him; she didn't know him because she suspected he didn't want to be known.

Gabby didn't think he would raise a hand to her. God knew he'd had plenty of reason to in the past, but he had never struck back at her in any way at all—apart from that kiss, of course. She had always secretly admired him for his self-restraint. She had been such a bitch towards him. How he had tolerated it still amazed her. So many young men in his position would have sought their revenge at the time; instead he had waited seven long years in order to do so...

Gabby gave a shiver and turned her attention back to her mother, who was crying into yet another crumpled tissue.

'It's OK, Mum,' she said gently. 'You heard what the surgeon said. Dad's going to be just fine.'

Pamela St Clair blew her nose. 'I know,

darling, but I just wish Blair was here,' she said. 'With your father out of action for God knows how long, what will happen to the business? Your father never tells me anything about what's going on. Are you sure it's all going well? You haven't said anything about it for ages, and I can't help worrying that…well, we could lose everything we've worked so hard for. If we were to lose the house… Oh, God, I just couldn't bear it!'

'Mum, stop worrying right now,' Gabby said, hugging her mother close so she couldn't see the deceit in her eyes. 'The resort is doing just fine. I spoke to the Fosters only yesterday. Everything is fine. They've had almost full occupancy for the last month. We're making a profit, just as we hoped and planned. Everything is safe and secure.'

'I'm so glad,' Pamela said, stepping back and wiping at her tears. 'I'm also glad about you marrying Vinn. I want you to know that, Gabby.'

Gabby met her mother's tawny-brown gaze. 'I always thought you didn't like him, Mum,' she said, trying not to frown. 'You always gave the impression he and his mother were beneath you.'

Pamela gave a wincing look. 'I know… It seems so…dreadfully hypocritical of me, thinking about it now,' she said. 'But I guess it was because I was so ashamed of my own background.'

Gabby allowed her frown purchase this time. 'What do you mean?'

Her mother blew her nose again and, tucking away the tissue, faced Gabby squarely. 'Darling, your father married me against his parents' wishes. We never spoke of it to you or to Blair, and thank God your grandparents when they were alive didn't mention anything either. But I was from the wrong side of the tracks, if you know what I mean.'

Gabby could barely believe her ears. She stood silently staring at her perfectly groomed mother, with her perfect diction and rounded vowels, and wondered if she had ever known her at all.

'Vinn's mother Rose reminded me of my own mother,' Pamela explained. 'She was an unwed mother too, with no skills to speak of, and at the mercy of whoever employed her. I was shunted from place to place for most of my childhood, never making friends long enough to keep them. As a result I dropped out of school and had to rely on my looks to get me where I wanted to go. I met your father at a function where I was waiting on tables. That's where I met Janice—Tristan's mother. Her parents owned the restaurant. She was so lovely to me, and we became close friends… The rest, as they say, is history.'

Gabby swallowed. 'You did love Dad when you married him, though, didn't you?' she asked, unconsciously holding her breath.

Pamela let out a long sigh and shifted her gaze. 'I didn't at first,' she confessed. 'The thing is I got pregnant with your brother. I was stupid and naive, and I didn't factor in the risks when we first started seeing each other. Your father insisted we marry, and so we did—against all the objections thrown at us.'

Gabby didn't say a word. Her voice seemed to be locked somewhere deep inside her throat.

Her mother's reddened eyes came back to hers. 'But over time I grew to love him. I don't have to tell you he is a good man, Gabby. He doesn't always get it right, any more than I do, but he's all I've got now apart from you. I just wish Blair h-hadn't…' She took a deep, uneven breath and continued, 'I just want you to be happy, Gabby. Janice, Tristan's mother, wishes it too. I was just talking to her last night. She and Gareth think the world of you. You were such a wonderful wife to their son.' She began to sob again, and buried her face into another wad of tissues.

Gabby felt sick. Guilt assailed her, almost over-whelming her already fragile control. Tristan's parents, like hers, had never known the full story. How could she have told them what had occurred behind closed doors? How could she have ruined so many lives by telling them the sordid truth?

She had felt so alone.

She *still* felt so alone.

Did anyone understand what it was like to carry such a burden of guilt and shame and regret? Would her life always be marked by the dark stains of her mistakes? How could she clear her slate and start afresh? Was it even possible?

Gabby became aware again of her mother's renewed bout of tears, and gathered her close. 'Don't cry, Mum,' she said softly. 'Things will work out. I know they will. Vinn and I will sort things out between us.'

Pamela brushed at her eyes as she removed herself from Gabby's embrace. 'Do you love him, darling?' she asked, looking at her intently.

Gabby felt her heart drop inside her chest. How could she lie to her own mother? Hadn't she already told so many lies? 'Um… Mum…' she faltered, shifting her gaze a fraction. 'What sort of question is that? Why on earth would I be marrying him if I didn't feel like…that for him?'

Her mother smiled a watery smile and, grasping Gabby's wrists, gripped them warmly. 'Then you will be a better wife to him than I was to your father in those first years of our marriage,' she said. 'At least you're not marrying

Vinn because you feel you have to. You are marrying him because you love him and can't imagine living your life with anyone else. Apart from Tristan, of course. You were soul mates—everyone knows that—but life throws up other paths, which is just as well, don't you think?'

Gabby stretched her mouth into a smile that felt as if it had been stitched in place. 'Of course,' she said. 'That's exactly what I think.'

When Gabby finally got home to Point Piper, Vinn arrived within minutes. As she checked his tall figure via the security camera, she wondered if he had been parked somewhere outside waiting for her.

He had called in at the hospital briefly, halfway through the afternoon, but hadn't stayed long. Just long enough to kiss her on the lips—a soft press of warm sensual flesh against her trembling mouth—before he turned and smiled at Gabby's mother. Gabby had listened to him chat about her father's condition with one ear while her heart had skipped and hopped all over the place and she'd surreptitiously swept her tongue where his mouth had just been. She had been able to taste him—a hint of good-quality coffee, a touch of mint, and a massive dose of sexy, full-blooded male.

Her belly had given a little quiver as she'd stood close to his side, his arm slipping around her waist in a possessive but strangely protective manner. She hadn't quite been able to control the instinct to move in even closer. He had felt so tall and strong, like a fortress.

Gabby had only suddenly realised her mother had left them to return to her father's bedside in ICU, where only one visitor was allowed at any time. She'd felt Vinn's arm drop from her waist and had quickly rearranged her features so he couldn't see how he had affected her.

'Do you think that kiss was necessary?' she asked, in a deliberately testy tone, taking great care not to glance at that sensual mouth, focussing on his grey-blue eyes instead.

His eyes contained a glint of amusement. 'Actually, I was thinking about slipping my tongue inside your mouth as well, but I thought your mother might be uncomfortable with such an obvious and very public display of my affection for her daughter.'

Gabby lifted her brows in twin arcs of cynicism. 'Affection?' she said. 'Is that what you call it? It's animal attraction, and you damn well know it.' She took a little heaving breath and added, 'And it's totally disgusting.'

He gave her a lazy smile and brushed the back of his hand down the side of her face—a barely touching caress, but it set off every nerve beneath the skin of her cheek like electrodes set on full voltage. 'Ah, but you feel it too, don't you, *mia piccola?*' he said. 'And soon we will be doing something about it, hmm?'

Gabby glowered at him even as she tried to ignore the flip-flop of her heart behind her breastbone. 'Not if I can help it,' she said stiffly, and crossed her arms tightly over her chest.

His smile widened and, leaning down, he pressed a soft-as-air kiss to her forehead before she could do anything to counteract it. 'Keep stoking that fiery passion of yours,' he drawled, in a low and sexy, knee-wobbling tone. 'I get turned on by the thought of you fighting me every step of the way, even though you want what I want. It's what you've always wanted.'

'I want you to burn in hell,' she bit out, practically shaking all over with rage.

He winked at her, and without another word turned and walked with those long easy strides of his down the corridor to the lifts.

Gabby stood watching him, annoyed with herself for doing so, but for some reason unable to get her body to move. The lift doors opened and she saw Vinn smile as two nurses came out, each one doing a swift double-take as he stepped into the lift. The doors whooshed shut behind him.

The nurses' voices carried as they came up the corridor towards Gabby. 'Wasn't that Vinn Venadicci?' the dark- haired one asked her redheaded companion. 'You know…the hotshot property investment tycoon?'

'Sure was,' the red head said. 'I heard a rumour he's just got engaged. His future father-in-law's just had open heart surgery. I wonder how long *that* marriage will last? Vinn Venadicci is a bit of a player, or so the gossip mags say.'

'I wouldn't mind a bit of a play with him,' the dark-haired nurse admitted with a grin. 'God, those eyes of his, and that smile would be enough to melt anyone's moral code.'

Gabby spun away in disgust and, pushing open the nearest female conveniences door, locked herself inside a cubicle until she was sure the nurses had moved on.

And now she had to face her nemesis all over again, Gabby thought sourly, as she opened the door of her parents' home to let Vinn in. She stepped well back, in case he took it upon himself to repeat his mode of greeting earlier that afternoon.

'Why are you here?' she asked in a clipped tone.

Vinn reached into the inside pocket of his suit jacket and handed her a black velvet box. 'This is for you,' he said, with an inscrutable expression. 'If you don't like the design you can exchange it for something else. It makes no difference to me.'

Gabby took the small box with an unsteady hand, desperately trying not to come into contact with his long fingers. But even so she felt the zap of his touch as one of her fingers brushed against one of his. She opened the lid and stared down at the classically designed solitaire diamond ring. The brilliance of the gem was absolutely breathtaking.

She looked up at him, her voice coming out slightly husky. 'It's…it's beautiful… It must have cost you a fortune.'

He gave her a wry look. 'Not quite as much as the margin call, but certainly close.'

Gabby pressed her lips together and looked at the diamond again, her mind reeling at the thought of how much he had paid for her to be his bride. Even though she had grown up with the sort of wealth and privilege most ordinary people never saw in a lifetime, she still couldn't quite believe the lengths Vinn was prepared to go to in order to secure her hand in marriage.

It made her realise yet again how difficult it was going to be for her to get out of the arrangement. She had already endured one miserable marriage, every day a torture of secrets and lies and betrayals. How would she cope with years of Vinn's philandering? He was sure to do so, since he had done little else since he had left the St Clair estate all those years ago.

'Of course you will have to remove Glendenning's rings first,' Vinn said into the silence.

Gabby looked down at her left hand, at the diamond cluster and the wedding band she had wanted to remove so many times over the last two years since Tristan's death. She'd felt unable to face the comments from her parents if she had done so.

'Yes…yes…of course,' she said, and began to tug at them.

One of Vinn's hands closed over hers, the other taking the velvet box out of her hand and putting it on a hall table next to him. 'Allow me,' he said. And, holding her left hand in the strength and warmth of his left one, he removed each of the rings, his grey-blue gaze not once leaving her startled brown one.

Gabby could feel her heart picking up its pace, and the way her breathing was becoming shallow and uneven. Her body felt hot inside and out—especially her hand, which was still enclosed in his. She took a tiny swallow as he reached for the ring he had bought her, and then her breathing stopped altogether as he gently eased the circle of white gold with its brilliant diamond along the slim length of her finger to its final resting place.

'It is a perfect fit,' he said with an enigmatic smile. 'How about that?'

Gabby couldn't account for her scattered emotions, but she felt as close to tears as she had the previous evening. It made her feel vulnerable in a way she resented feeling in front of someone she disliked so intensely.

'A lucky guess,' she said in an off-hand tone, and stepped back from him.

A flicker of annoyance momentarily darkened the blue in his eyes. 'Are you going to invite me in for a drink to celebrate our impending marriage?' he asked. 'If so, I think I might remove my shirt right now, in case you take it upon yourself to throw the contents of your glass at me again.'

Gabby tightened her mouth like the strings of an evening purse. 'I promise not to throw anything at you if you promise to keep your insulting suppositions to yourself,' she said, with an elevation of her chin.

'And what would some of those suppositions be, I wonder?' he mused.

She stalked towards the large lounge overlooking the harbour, tossing over her shoulder, 'What would you like to drink? We have the usual

spirits and mixers, wine and champagne—
French, even, if you so desire it.'

'I think you know very well what I desire,
Gabriella,' he said, as he came to where she
was standing in front of the bar fridge and
drinks servery.

Gabby sucked in a sharp little breath as his
hands came down on the tops of her shoulders.
The heat of his touch was like a brand, even
through the layer of her cotton shirt. She felt the
solid presence of him at her back, and wondered
what it would feel like to lean back into his
hardness, to feel the hard outline of his body
against the softness of hers, to feel his hands
move from her shoulders to cup her breasts, to
feel the slight abrasion of his fingers skating over
her erect nipples…

She might not like him, but Gabby was starting
to realise she would be lying to herself if she said
she didn't desire him. He had a magnetism about
him that was totally enthralling. Even now she
felt an overwhelming compulsion to turn around

and lock gazes with him, to see if his need was anything like her own.

'What's that perfume you are wearing?' he asked, moving in a little closer.

Gabby felt her spine give a distinct wobble as his chest rumbled against her back as he spoke. 'Um...I'm not sure... I can't remember... Something I've had for ages...' She couldn't seem to get her scrambled brain to work. It seemed to be short-circuited by all her body was feeling with him so close.

'It reminds me of warm summer nights,' he said against the shell of her ear. 'Frangipani and jasmine and something else.'

Gabby wondered if the 'something else' was the scent of her desire for him. She could feel silky moisture gathering between her thighs, the secret and hollow ache making her feel even more unguarded around him. She had always been able to hold him off with her caustic tongue. That had been her protection in the past. But what if her body totally betrayed her now? Could he sense how close she was to responding to the temptation of his closeness?

Vinn turned her around to face him, his hands sliding down the length of her slender arms, his right thumb rolling over the bump of the diamond ring on her finger, back and forth, as he watched the way her expression became shuttered, as if his touch didn't affect her one iota. But he could feel the slight tremble of her hands in his, and see the flare of her pupils, making her toffee-brown eyes darken, and the way the point of her tongue darted out to deposit a fine layer of moisture over her soft lips.

He wanted to kiss her, to taste the sweetness of her, to feel her tongue war with his until he tamed it. He wanted to press her back against the nearest wall and bury himself in her, to feel his hard body surrounded by her silky warmth, to thrust himself to paradise and take her writhing and screaming with him.

But instead he released her hands and stepped back from her. 'I have changed my mind about that drink,' he said. 'I have another engagement this evening, and since I drove myself here instead of using a cab, I don't want to end up with a drink-driving charge.'

A frown pulled at her smooth brow. 'You don't have a driver?' she asked.

'Not a full-time one,' he said. 'And nor do I have a live-in housekeeper, so I hope it's not going to be a problem for you pitching in occasionally to help keep things running smoothly at home.'

Her frown deepened, and a fiery light came into her eyes as they narrowed slightly. 'Is this some sort of sick joke?' she asked.

'It's no joke, Blondie,' he said. 'I do my own cooking, and I expect you to do the same.'

'B-but you're a multi-millionaire for God's sake!' she spluttered. 'In fact, aren't you close to being a billionaire by now?'

'So?'

'So you get people to do stuff for you,' she said, flapping her hands for effect. 'It's totally crazy, spending your time on menial tasks when you could employ someone else to do it for you so you can concentrate on what you're best at doing.'

'I happen to enjoy cooking,' Vinn said, relishing every second of their exchange. She was so pampered she hadn't a clue how the real world worked, and it would do her good to learn. It would teach her to think twice about treating those less fortunate than her with her customary disdain.

'If you think for one minute I'm going to wash your socks and fold your underwear then you are even more deluded than I thought,' she tossed at him heatedly.

'The only thing I expect you to do with my underwear is peel it off me—preferably with your teeth,' he returned with a deliberately lascivious look.

Her eyes flared and he saw her hands go to tight little fists by her sides. 'I will do no such thing!'

He gave a chuckle of laughter and, before he was tempted to kiss that pouting mouth of hers, turned on his heel and left.

Gabby stormed up and down the lounge after

he had driven away, her anger duelling with her disappointment that he hadn't stayed for a drink.

No, that wasn't quite the truth, she decided on her pace back towards the sofa. What she had really wanted him to do was to stay long enough to kiss her. She had been expecting him to turn her around in his arms and smother her mouth with his. Her whole body had been screaming out for it. But he had left her high and dry. She hated him for it. She hated him for toying with her like a cat with a mouse, taunting it, teasing it mercilessly, just waiting for the best moment to make that final devastating pounce.

She hated him.

OK, so that wasn't quite the truth either, Gabby thought as she scraped her fingers through her hair. That was the whole problem. She didn't know what the hell she felt for Vinn Venadicci, but one thing was certain: it was not as close to hate as she wanted and most desperately needed it to be.

CHAPTER SIX

'DARLING,' Pamela St Clair said to Gabby as soon as she arrived at the hospital the following morning. 'Please tell me this…this…' she thrust the morning's newspaper in Gabby's hands '…this scandalmongering isn't true!'

Gabby looked at the page the newspaper was folded open to and felt a knife-like pain jab through her. There was a photograph of Vinn with his arm around a young and very beautiful brunette, who was smiling up at him adoringly. The couple of paragraphs accompanying the picture declared Vinn Venadicci was rumoured to be getting married to widowed socialite Gabriella Glendenning, nee St Clair, and the journalist was quite adamant the young woman with him was not his fiancée but a mystery date he had been seen with once or twice before.

'Well?' Pamela St Clair was practically wringing her hands. 'For God's sake, Gabby, if your father hears or sees this it could cause another heart attack.'

'Mum…' Somehow Gabby located her voice, but it sounded slightly strangled. 'Of course it's not true. You know what the press are like. They make this stuff up all the time. It's probably an old photo.'

Pamela's eyes narrowed. 'Are you sure?' she asked. 'Are you absolutely sure?'

Gabby had never felt more uncertain in her life, but she was not going to admit that to her mother. With an acting skill she had no idea she had possessed until now, she relaxed her tense features into a smile and handed back the paper with a surprisingly steady hand. 'Mum,' she said, holding out her left hand, 'do you think Vinn would give me this and then go off gallivanting with someone else the very same evening?'

Her mother gasped as she held Gabby's hand

up to the light. 'Oh, my God, it's gorgeous,' she said. 'It must have cost him an arm and a leg.'

Gabby took her hand back. 'Yes, it did,' she said, unconsciously fingering the diamond. 'But apparently I'm worth it.'

Pamela looked past Gabby's shoulder. 'Oh… Vinn…' She cleared her throat delicately and continued, 'We were…er…just talking about you.'

Gabby had to summon even more acting ability to face Vinn with any sense of equanimity. 'Hi,' she said, and reached up on tiptoe to plant a brief kiss on his cheek, with the intention of landing it close enough to his mouth for her mother to be fooled. However Vinn had other ideas. He took control of her mouth in a deep, bone-melting assault on her senses that left her totally out of kilter once it ended.

'Hi yourself, *cara*,' he said, before turning to face Gabby's mother, who was trying to hide the newspaper behind her back but failing miserably. 'I hope you weren't upset by that article? I have already spoken to my legal advisors about lodging a defamation claim against the journalist concerned.'

'Oh...' Pamela said, smiling broadly. 'No... no, of course not, Vinn. I wasn't upset at all, and neither was Gabby. Were you, darling?'

Gabby smiled stiffly. 'I am well used to the mudslinging that goes on in the press, having been subjected to it myself once or twice in the past.'

Vinn smiled as if butter wouldn't melt on his skin, let alone in his mouth, Gabby thought resentfully.

'So how is Henry doing today?' he asked, addressing Pamela.

'He's resting just now, but he's had a good night,' Pamela answered with visible relief. 'The surgeon is pleased with everything so far. It's just important we keep him quiet and free from stress.'

'Yes, of course,' Vinn said, reaching for Gabby's hand and pulling her closer. 'We'll let you get back to him while we have a coffee together. Can I get you something before we go?'

Pamela blushed like a schoolgirl. 'Oh, no, I'm

fine, thank you, Vinn,' she said and then started to gush like one too. 'You're so kind. You've been absolutely marvellous. Gabby's so lucky to have someone like you. I really mean it. And that ring! Why, it's practically the Hope Diamond!'

Vinn gave a low rumble of laughter. 'Not quite—but she's worth it, don't you think?'

Pamela beamed from ear to ear. 'Well, she's my daughter, so I have to agree, don't I? But she *is* worth it—although it would please me to see her smile a bit more. Come on, darling.' She swung her gaze to Gabby. 'I must say for someone who is supposed to be madly in love you don't seem all that happy.'

'Um… I'm just worried about Dad, that's all,' Gabby faltered. 'It's been such a trying time and…'

Vinn's arm snaked around Gabby's waist. 'I promise you, Mrs St Clair, you won't know her when I bring her back from our honeymoon,' he said. 'She will be smiling from ear to ear. I guarantee it.'

Pamela blushed again. 'Oh, my, but you have

turned into such a charmer, Vinn Venadicci. And you really must call me Pamela now that you're to be part of the family.'

'Thank you, Pamela,' he said, with an easy-going smile.

Gabby pulled herself out of his hold once her mother had gone back to be with her father. 'Who is she?' she threw at him icily.

'Who is who?' Vinn asked, as he began leading the way down the corridor towards the lifts.

Gabby had to trot to keep up. 'That woman in the picture,' she said, glancing around to see if anyone was listening. 'She's your mistress, isn't she?' she hissed at him in a hushed tone. 'Don't bother denying it, because I just won't believe you.'

He pressed the 'down' button. 'Then I won't waste my time denying it,' he said. 'What would be the point, if you're not going to believe me either way?'

Gabby glared at him as they stepped into the lift, but couldn't fling a retort his way due to several other passengers in the lift. She stood stiffly by his side, her anger towards him going upwards even as the floor numbers went downwards.

The lift delivered them on the ground floor, and Vinn placed a hand beneath her elbow to guide her out of the busy hospital foyer to where his car was parked.

'Where are we going?' Gabby asked, flinging him a churlish look.

'We are going to have a coffee together,' he said, and opened the passenger door for her. 'Get in.'

She threw him another furious glare. 'Don't order me about as if I'm a child.'

'Then don't act like one,' he returned, and repeated his command, this time with an implacable edge to his tone. 'Get in the car.'

'I don't see why we have to drive somewhere to have a coffee when there's a perfectly good cafeteria back there in the hospital foyer,' she tossed back, with a shrug of her shoulders.

Vinn's eyes challenged hers. 'You know something, Blondie?' he said. 'You are really starting to annoy me—and that is not a good thing.'

'Yeah, well, you're a late starter then, because I've been annoyed with you from the moment I met you,' she threw back, her brown eyes flashing at him.

Vinn put the brakes on his temper with an effort. 'Listen,' he said, 'I have nothing against hospital food and drink, but right now I want us to be alone. We have things to discuss.'

She gave him a contentious look. 'Like your mystery lover?'

Vinn silently ground his teeth. 'She is nothing of the sort. She's a…friend.'

Her brows lifted cynically. 'A friend, huh?' she said. 'What do you take me for, Vinn? Do you think I'm so naive I would fall for that old line?'

Vinn set his mouth. 'Quite frankly, right at this minute I don't give a damn *what* you think,' he bit out. 'I have a huge list of things to see to today because I'm going to be away next week, and I can do without this infantile behaviour from you—especially considering the money I've handed over without a single word of thanks from you.'

'You expect me to *thank* you for blackmailing me into marriage?' she asked in an incredulous tone.

'If you're not happy with the conditions you can hand back the money and the ring,' he said, locking his eyes on hers. 'Right here and right now.'

Gabby tussled for a moment with his challenging and annoyingly confident look. There was no point calling his bluff because there was no way she could find an alternative source of funds to keep the resort safe. 'You know I can't do that…' she mumbled.

'Then let's go with Plan A and get on with it,' he said and nodded his head towards the passenger seat.

Gabby got in the car with uncharacteristic meekness, her spirits sagging. Her head was starting to pound from the tension in her neck and shoulders that had been building all morning. She pressed her fingers to the bridge of her nose, her eyes scrunched closed to avoid the stab of bright sunlight coming through the windscreen.

'Hey…' Vinn's deep voice was almost as soothing as the warmth of his palm at the back of her neck, the gentle massaging of his fingers untying the knots of tension like magic. 'You have a headache, yes?'

She bit her lip and gave a tiny nod. 'I didn't sleep well, and I skipped breakfast…'

She heard him mutter a curse, but his fingers didn't stop their soothing action. She rolled her head and shoulders to make the most of his touch, her breath coming out in a long, easy stream as the tension gradually eased.

'Feeling a bit better?' he asked.

She opened her eyes and turned to look at him, her heart stalling like an old engine. There was concern in his grey-blue gaze, and his mouth had lost its grim set. He was now looking as sensually tempting and irresistible as ever. She couldn't seem to stop looking at him, at the way his mouth tipped up at the corners as if he always had a smile at the ready, the fuller bottom lip hinting at the potent sensuality of his nature.

Then there was the dark stubble that peppered his jaw, in spite of his early-morning shave, making him so essentially masculine she wanted to place the palm of her hand on his face and feel the texture of his skin, feel the abrasion of it against her softer one. She could imagine herself kissing her way all over his face, over each of the dark slashes of his eyebrows, his eyelids, and down the length of his crooked patrician nose until she got to his lips.

Gabby felt her eyelids begin to lower as his mouth came inexorably closer, his head tilting to accommodate the contours of their faces. The slow-motion brush of his lips against hers was soft, like a feather floating down to land on top of a smooth surface. Her lips tingled from the brief contact, each nerve springing to life in anticipation of a follow-up kiss.

But instead he sat back in the driver's seat and started the engine with a throaty roar. Releasing the handbrake, he sent her a smile before turning back to the task of driving out of the car park.

Gabby rolled her lips together, to see if it would stop them tingling, but all it did was make her hungry for more of his drugging kisses. Was he doing it on purpose? she wondered. Day by day ramping up her desire for him, so she would not be able to resist him when he decided it was time to consummate their marriage. Her belly quivered at the thought of him making love to her, his hands on her body, touching her, stroking and caressing her until she was boneless with need.

She fidgeted in her seat, her body hot and bothered, and that secret place between her thighs pulsing and aching and moist with want.

Would she disappoint him? In spite of her marriage to Tristan she had never experienced pleasure, only pain and shame. She mentally cringed as she recalled the filthy insults her late husband had flung at her, making her feel so worthless and unattractive the little self-esteem she had possessed had been obliterated completely.

Gabby suddenly became aware of where they were heading as Vinn took the exit to Mosman off the Harbour Bridge. 'We're going to your house?' she asked, swivelling to look at him.

'Yes,' he said, concentrating on the traffic. 'We could have gone to a café in the city, but you obviously need some peace and quiet—not to mention a couple of painkillers.'

Gabby turned back to look at the road ahead, her brow creasing slightly. The caring, solicitous Vinn was a change from the teasing, taunting one, but she wondered if he was trying to divert her attention away from his mystery lover by acting out the role of thoughtful fiancé. Jealousy gnawed at her insides like hundreds of miniature hungry mouths nipping at her tender flesh, making her feel sick with despair.

She didn't want to feel such intensity of emotion.

She didn't want to feel vulnerable.

She suddenly realised with a little jolt of surprise she didn't want him to want anyone else. She wanted him to want her and only her.

Vinn parked the car in the driveway and strode around to help her out of her side. She looked pale, and there were dark bruise-like shadows under her eyes. Her mouth had a downward turn to it. It was obvious she was burning the candle at both ends, spending long hours at the hospital as well as juggling her father's business affairs.

He was all too familiar with the worry over an ill parent. Watching his beloved mother die had been one of the toughest things he had ever faced, made all the harder when he had received the news of Blair St Clair's suicide. Vinn hadn't been able to leave his mother's bedside and travel to the other side of the globe to attend Blair's funeral. Nor had he been able to offer much in the way of support to Blair's parents and Gabriella, even though he had dearly wanted to.

The news of her engagement a few weeks after Blair's death had been another blow he had struggled to deal with. He had never particularly liked Tristan Glendenning; there had always been something about him that irked Vinn the more he got to know him. He'd been too smooth, too self-assured, and not one bit in love with

Gabriella. Of that Vinn was sure. But in spite of his warning she had married Glendenning anyway. And the bruisers Tristan had engaged to work him over had certainly kept him away from the wedding, as Gabriella had requested. Vinn had put up a tough fight, but four against one was asking too much—even of someone with his level of physical fitness.

Vinn escorted her inside the house and straight to the kitchen, where he pulled out a stool for her. 'Sit,' he said. 'I'll make you some scrambled eggs and toast.'

For a moment or two she looked as if she was about to refuse, but then she gave a little sigh and wriggled onto the stool. 'Don't make too much,' she said. 'I'm not really very hungry.'

'When was the last time you ate?' he asked as he placed a knob of butter in the pan and set it on the cooktop.

'I don't know… I can't remember,' she said. 'Lunch yesterday?'

He rolled his eyes as he reached for a carton of

eggs in the fridge. 'If you get any slimmer you'll have to wear snow skis in the shower to stop you going down the drain.'

She gave him a droll look. 'Very funny.'

Vinn cracked some eggs into a bowl and began to whisk them. 'How are you the handling work at the office since your father's been taking a break?' he asked, in a casually interested tone.

The momentary silence made him glance at her over his shoulder. 'Not so good, huh?' he said.

'What makes you think that?' she said with a defensive set to her features. 'You think I'm not capable of handling things on my own?'

He gave the eggs a good grind of pepper before responding. 'My gut feeling is you only do it because you feel you have something to prove. Your heart's not in it. It's never been in it.'

Her silence this time was a fraction longer. Vinn could almost hear the cogs of her brain ticking over, trying to find some way of justifying herself.

'It's a family business,' she said at last.

'So?'

'So family members usually take up some sort of role in the company.'

'Yes,' he said. 'But it helps if they're suited for it. And it helps even more if they enjoy it and get some sort of satisfaction out of it.'

He turned to see her slip down off the stool, her arms going across her chest in that classic defensive pose. 'I do enjoy it,' she said, but her eyes skittered away from his.

'Perhaps. But I still think there are things you would enjoy more.'

'Oh, really?' Gabby said, flashing her gaze back to his. 'Since when have you become such an expert on what would satisfy me?'

His eyes gave her that look—the look that made Gabby's legs feel weak and watery and her belly start to flutter as if tiny wings were beating with excitement inside her. And then her colour rose as she realised she could have phrased her question with perhaps a little less propensity for a double meaning.

'Because I know you, Gabriella,' he said. 'You have no head for business. And I'm not the only one who thinks so.'

Gabby stiffened as she looked at him. 'What?' she said, narrowing her eyes in suspicion. 'You mean you've been talking to someone in the company about me?'

He leaned back against the bench in an indolent manner. 'I just poured two point four million dollars into the company. Did you think I wouldn't do a bit of research before I committed myself so heavily?'

'What sort of research did you do?' Gabby asked with a guarded look. 'It's not like you had much time. I came to see you practically at the last minute, and you—' She stopped, her heart beginning to pound as the truth began to dawn. 'You went snooping around well before then, though, didn't you? My God, but you have some gall, Vinn Venadicci. How dare you undermine me like that?'

'I was concerned about your father's health

way before he had the heart attack,' he said. 'I had lunch with him a couple of months ago and it became clear to me he didn't have his finger on the pulse of the business any more. He had lost that fire in his belly. Quite frankly, I think he was relieved to leave you in charge because he was feeling so worn out. It's my bet that once he recovers he'll change his mind about retiring and want to get back at the helm—which is why I have organised a business manager to take your place until he does. He starts tomorrow.'

Gabby's eyes went wide in outrage. 'You did *what*?'

'I want you to take a break from the business,' he said, dishing up the eggs. 'Take a few months to think about what you'd like to do. You might find you'd prefer not to work at all and just enjoy being a wife and mother.'

She gave him a livid glare. 'You've got it all worked out, haven't you, Vinn? You expect me to give up everything just to be a breeding machine. God, I can't believe there are still men like you around. I thought they died out with the dinosaurs.'

He set the plate of eggs and toast on the bench between them. 'Sit down and eat that before it gets cold,' he said.

In a fit of temper Gabby shoved the plate back towards him, with more force than she had really intended. The plate slid off the bench and shattered on the floor at his feet, eggs and toast going everywhere.

Her eyes flew to his in apprehension. 'I—I'm sorry,' she said. 'I didn't mean to do that…'

'Sure you didn't.' He stepped back from the mess, his eyes hard on hers, his mouth pulled into a tight line of simmering anger.

Gabby took an unsteady step backwards. 'I'll c-clean it up,' she said, in a voice that was scratchy and uneven. 'If you'll just show me where the dustpan and broom are…'

'Leave it,' he said tersely. 'I'll see to it myself. In any case, you probably wouldn't know one end of a broom from the other.'

She compressed her lips, struggling to keep the tears back but in the end failing. One by one they slipped past the shield of her lashes and silently flowed down her cheeks.

Vinn paused on his way back from the utilities cupboard with the dustpan and broom. 'It's just a plate of eggs,' he said, his anger fading at the sight of her tears. 'It's not the end of the world.'

She choked back a sob and covered her face with her hands, her shoulders shaking as she began to cry in earnest.

He let out a little curse, directed at himself rather than her, and, putting the pan and broom to one side, gathered her in his arms. 'Are you *sure* it's not that time of the month?' he asked.

She shook her head, buried against his chest, and sobbed and sniffled some more.

He stroked his fingers through the silky strands of her blonde hair, enjoying the feel of her soft and pliant against him. Her sobs gradually died down until she was silent, her head turned sideways, so her cheek was pressed close to his thudding heart.

His body was getting harder by the second, and the rush of blood to his groin was making him ache to grind his pelvis against hers. He could feel the softness of her breasts pressing against his chest, and her arms had somehow snaked around his waist, bringing her lower body just that little bit closer to his.

He felt a tremor of awareness go through her, like little ripples over the surface of smooth water, and then she lifted her head and met his gaze, her lips so soft and inviting that he brought his head down and covered them with his own.

CHAPTER SEVEN

GABBY totally melted under the blowtorch of his kiss. His lips were hard and then soft, firm and demanding one minute, gentle and cajoling the next. It was a heady repertoire, making all her senses shiver in response.

She returned his kiss with a level of passion that was almost frightening in its intensity. She was on fire for him, every part of her longing to feel him touch her all over, to bring her body to the highest peak of pleasure. She felt the stirring of her intimate muscles, the liquid warmth that seeped from deep inside her to prepare her for the thick invasion of his body. She could feel how aroused he was—so very hard, so intoxicatingly male.

With his mouth still locked on hers, Gabby felt

his fingers working on the tiny buttons of her cotton top, undoing them one by one as his tongue danced a sexy tango with hers. He didn't bother undoing her bra; he simply shoved it out of the way and bent his mouth to her breast. She gasped in delight as his tongue circled her nipple a couple of times, before he began to suckle on her with a gentle drawing-in motion that made her knees start to buckle. He moved to her other breast, increasing the pressure of his mouth, using his teeth in tiny tug-like bites that sent shooting sparks of need right through her core. Waves of pleasure rolled over her, making her mind empty of everything but how he was making her feel.

He brought his mouth back to hers in a scorching kiss of passionate urgency, his pelvis jammed so tightly against hers she felt the throb and thunder of his blood beneath his skin.

'You taste so damned good,' he said, just above her swollen lips. 'I want to taste all of you— every beautiful inch of you.'

Gabby reconnected her mouth to his, her tongue stroking and curling around his, tasting the maleness and fiery heat of him. Her heart-rate went through the roof as he nudged her thighs apart, rubbing one of his own against her feminine mound. Her body exploded with sensation, the deep hollow ache intensifying until she was whimpering, soft little mewing sounds that came from the back of her throat.

'Come upstairs with me,' he said, lifting his mouth again to look down at her, his grey-blue eyes as dark as she had ever seen them. 'We don't have to wait until Friday. I want you now.'

Gabby felt herself wavering. Her body was tilting her one way while her brain was trying desperately to send her back the other. He had a mistress, she reminded herself. He was a playboy. He was only marrying her for revenge. There was no love in the arrangement—not even mild affection. This was about lust. He had wanted her for a long time and had gone to extraordinary lengths to have her. He would use her, and when he grew tired of her she would be left, trapped in a going-nowhere marriage, until he decided if or when it was to end.

Her body put up an equally powerful argument. It was still throbbing with need, every pore of her skin sensitised to his touch, every nerve-ending buzzing. Her lips were as swollen as the folds of her feminine cleft, the silky moisture between them making it even harder to ignore the need he had awakened in her.

'Or what about we do it here?' Vinn said, spinning her round so her back was against the kitchen bench. One of his hands lifted her skirt, his fingers searching for her moist heat.

'No!' Gabby thrust both hands against his chest.

He cocked one brow at her, his hand stilling on her thigh. 'No?'

She pressed her lips together, trying to control her breathing, trying to tame her wild needs, trying to gather some sense of decency and self-respect.

'No...' she said, releasing a tightly held breath. 'I can't...'

'You certainly weren't giving me that impression a few seconds ago,' he pointed out, with more than a hint of wryness. 'May I ask what changed your mind?'

Gabby moved out of his hold, rearranging her clothing with as much dignity as was possible, considering her breasts were bare and still damp from the ministrations of his mouth.

'I don't want to sleep with you before we get married,' she said, saying the first thing that came into her mind.

'For God's sake, Gabriella, you've been married for to another man, so it's not as if you're some sweet virgin saving yourself for your wedding night.'

Gabby could hear the frustration in his voice, and felt guilty and ashamed for allowing things to go as far as they had. 'I'm sorry… I know it's hard for you…'

He gave a rough bark of laughter. '*Hard* being the operative word.'

She felt colour storm into her cheeks and bit

down on her lip. 'This is not easy for me,' she said, still fumbling with her buttons. 'It's…it's been a long time since I…you know…was intimate with…with—'

He placed a finger over her lips, his eyes a steely grey. 'Let's not keep bringing your late husband into the conversation, hmm? Every time I think of you with him I want to punch something.'

She stood there, her mouth sealed with his fingertip, the desire to push her tongue out to meet it almost overwhelming.

After a tense moment his finger dropped from her lips. 'Was he your first lover?' he asked.

Gabby gave a tiny nod, mentally grimacing as she recalled the one and only time Tristan had forced himself on her. She had never thought it would be that painful—but then he had not done anything to prepare her. She had been used like a whore and left torn apart, both physically and emotionally.

'Has there been anyone since?' Vinn asked, after another short but tense silence.

She shook her head. 'No… No one…'

He wondered whether or not to believe her. She certainly hadn't grieved the way everyone had expected her to grieve. Her husband had wrapped himself around a telegraph pole on his way home from work on the night of their fifth anniversary, dying instantly—or so the coroner had found. The press had captured Gabriella numerous times in the first few weeks after Glendenning's death, carrying on as if nothing had happened. She had shopped, got her highlights and nails done, with nary a hint of sadness etched on her beautiful face. Vinn had often wondered if the rumours he had heard around town were true. Word had it she'd had numerous affairs during her marriage, and that Glendenning had chosen to turn a blind eye rather than jeopardise the alliance of the two well-to-do family empires.

'Did you love him?' Vinn asked.

'I thought you didn't want me to talk about him?' she said, with an ironic glance over her shoulder.

'It's a simple question,' he said. 'And, like most simple questions, a yes or no will suffice.'

'Why do you want to know?' she asked, turning to face him. 'It's not as if you have any feelings for me other than lust. Or are you not telling me something I should know?'

Vinn had to admire her talent for the quick comeback. She was good at getting the focus off herself. The funny thing was, he wasn't exactly sure what he felt about her. For years he had simultaneously desired and hated her. She had been such a toffee-nosed bitch to him in the past, and while he could forgive those misdemeanours on the basis of her youth at the time, he could not forgive her for the way she still looked down her nose at him now. To her he was still the house-cleaner's son—not worthy to hold a door open for her let alone touch her until she screamed his name in ecstasy as he was so determined she would do.

'That would suit you, now, wouldn't it, Gabriella?' he said. 'To get me to confess undying love for you? Sorry to disappoint you, but my feelings are much more basic. Lust is a good word. Perhaps a little coarse for someone from your rather cosseted background, but it more or less sums it up.'

She gave him a haughty glare.

He smiled as he picked up his car keys. 'You might want to rebutton your top, Blondie, before I take you back to the hospital to see your father. The last button doesn't seem to have found its correct hole.'

Gabby looked down at her shirt and felt her face fire up. She looked as dishevelled and as ravished as she felt—but, even worse, Vinn had yet again got in the last word. She felt as if he had her pride in the palm of his hand and with just one small clench of his fist he could totally destroy it. She was going to fight tooth and nail to stop that from happening, but with each kiss he subjected her to she realised she was drifting further and further out of her depth and into totally unchartered waters.

She had always thought marrying Tristan

Glendenning had been the biggest mistake of her life, but she could see now that falling in love with Vinn Venadicci would more than likely surpass it in spades.

Gabby stood by Vinn's side in front of the marriage celebrant and listened to herself mechanically repeat the vows that under the circumstances were nothing short of meaningless.

Vinn's clear and deep voice, however, made them sound much more convincing, she thought. The way he spoke with such firm conviction sounded as if he did indeed love her, and would treat her with honour and respect for the rest of their lives.

She turned when the celebrant said it was time for him to kiss the bride, and, tipping up her face, closed her eyes as Vinn's mouth sealed hers with a kiss that had a hint of possessiveness about it. Each movement of his lips on hers seemed to say, *You are mine now, body and soul.* And Gabby knew if Vinn had his way that could very well be the case within a matter of hours.

Their flights had been booked for their trip to the St Clair Island Resort, and they were due to leave within just over an hour. Their luggage was already in Vinn's car, and once the marriage certificate was signed he escorted Gabby out to where it was parked on the street outside.

Gabby found it hard to think of something to say on the way to the airport. She was conscious of Vinn's muscled arm occasionally shifting gears near her thigh. He had already taken off his jacket and peeled back his shirt cuffs due to the increase in temperature. The ink-black springy hairs on his forearms made her feel a mixture of trepidation and excitement to feel his touch on her bare skin.

There would be plenty of opportunity to do so on the tropical island resort, she reminded herself, with another little quiver of nervous anticipation. She had looked at next week's weather forecast, and with temperatures in the late twenties and low thirties predicted on the island, she knew her bikini and sarong would be the most she would be wearing during the day. She didn't dare think what she would be wearing at night. If Vinn had his way she was sure she would be naked.

'How long has it been since you were last on the island?' Vinn's voice cut across her thoughts.

Gabby had to think for a moment. 'I flew up earlier in the year,' she said. 'February, I think it was. I went up to check over the new refurbishment, but I only stayed a couple of nights.'

He didn't say anything in response, but Gabby wondered if he thought she should have visited more often, to keep a closer eye on things. The new business manager he had appointed had already found a few mistakes in her records, which had increased Gabby's feelings of incompetence, although Vinn had not made a big issue of it at the time. He had simply told Mark Vella that things had been very stressful recently. with Gabriella's father's health issues, and Gabby had found herself hoping he was doing it for the sake of her feelings. But she had realised in a saner moment he had probably been playing the part of supportive fiancé again, and her feelings had not been a consideration of his at all.

She was not quite ready to admit it to Vinn, but since she had stopped going into the office she had felt as if a huge weight had been lifted off her shoulders. Even her parents had not been the least bit concerned when she had stepped down from the board. Instead they had both communicated how much they trusted Vinn's judgement in handling the business side of things while Henry was out of action.

'Anyway,' her mother had said with a coy smile, 'it won't be long before we hear the patter of tiny feet, I am sure. Right, Gabby? After all, you are getting on for thirty. You don't want to leave it too late to have children, otherwise you might miss out altogether.'

Vinn had smiled as he'd placed his arm around Gabby's waist. 'Don't worry, Pamela,' he'd said. 'We'll get working on it right away.'

Gabby had blushed to the roots of her hair, but

had forced a stiff smile to her face. She had, however, given Vinn's arm a hard pinch, and sent him a reproachful glare when her parents hadn't been looking. But all he had done was wink at her, which had made her already simmering blood start to boil.

Vinn drove into the valet parking area at the airport, and within in a few minutes they were checked in and waiting to board.

Once they were on their way the flight gave Gabby the perfect opportunity to close her eyes and feign sleep. But after what seemed just a few minutes she opened her eyes to find herself leaning against Vinn's shoulder.

She straightened and blinked a couple of times. 'Sorry…I must have fallen asleep,' she said. 'I hope I didn't crease your shirt too much.'

His smile was easy and relaxed. 'No, it's fine. I enjoyed listening to you snore, actually.'

Gabby pursed her lips. 'I do not snore.'

'How would you know?' he asked with the arch of one brow. 'You haven't had a lover since your husband passed away, or so you said.'

She frowned at him. 'Don't you believe me?'

He looked at her for a lengthy moment. 'You cannot be unaware of the rumours that circulated during your marriage.'

Gabby felt her stomach drop. 'W-what rumours?'

His gaze continued to pin hers. 'Rumours about all the lovers you took.'

Gabby felt her cheeks grow warm under his piercing scrutiny. 'I find it rather ironic that you apparently take on board everything you read in the press when you insisted that the woman you were photographed with was not your mistress when everything pointed to her being so.'

'So you are saying the rumours about you were unfounded?' he asked, still looking at her unwaveringly.

Gabby wondered if she should tell him what had really gone on during her marriage. But two things stopped her. One was the fact they were sitting on a plane surrounded by other people, and the other was her pride. Vinn had been the one to warn her not to marry Tristan, and she had ignored that warning and paid for it dearly. She couldn't risk him rubbing her nose in it every chance he could. She had suffered enough. In some ways she would always suffer for that mistake. Her life had taken on a trajectory she could never have anticipated.

'I am saying you shouldn't believe every bit of gossip you hear,' she said. 'There are always two sides to every story.'

'I have heard there are three,' he said with an enigmatic smile. 'The wife's version, the husband's version, and then there's the truth.'

Gabby was relieved when the flight attendant announced they were preparing to land at that point, so she didn't have to continue the conversation. She pushed her handbag back under the seat in front and, tightening her seatbelt, looked out of the window at the azure blue of the ocean below.

Various other tourist islands were dotted

around St Clair Island, but to Gabby none of them seemed as beautiful and tranquil. She had fond memories of coming to the island as a child. She had spent so many magical days with her brother, beachcombing, making sandcastles and sand sculptures, going for walks to all the private beaches away from the main one at the front of the resort restaurant and bar area.

A wave of nostalgia came over Gabby as the plane touched down. She felt tears spring to her eyes, and had to blink rapidly to make them go away. Blair had loved the island as much as she did. Even after all this time it was still hard to imagine he would never come here again, and walk with her along the sandy shore to pick up a shell or two to add to his collection.

Vinn's hand reached for one of hers, where it was clasped tightly in her lap, his long fingers curling around her smaller ones. 'Everything all right?' he asked.

Gabby gave him a forced smile. 'Of course. It was just a bumpy landing, that's all.'

He gave her fingers an almost imperceptible squeeze. 'I miss him too, *cara*. He was a good friend,' he said softly.

Gabby's throat thickened, but she somehow managed to speak in spite of it. 'You were like a brother to him. I was so jealous of how well you got on. It seems so petty and childish now…'

'You *were* a child,' he said, releasing her fingers. 'And a rather spoilt one at that. I am not going to hold it against you.'

Gabby surreptitiously massaged her fingers where his touch had set off a tingling reaction beneath her skin, all the time wondering if what he had said was true. Wasn't that the whole point of their marriage?

Retribution.

Revenge.

Vengeance…

She gave a little involuntary shiver as the last word and its well-worn biblical phrase reverberated in her head.

Vengeance is mine…

CHAPTER EIGHT

THE resort managers, Judy and Garry Foster, gave Vinn and Gabby a warm welcome. Garry took their luggage ahead, and, after a little tour of the resort for Vinn's benefit, Judy led the way to their deluxe penthouse-style unit overlooking its own private beach.

There was a plunge pool and a spa and sauna, and an outdoor shower with twin shower heads set in a tropical garden that was totally private. The exotic fragrance of frangipani was heavy in the warm air, and each of the bright splashes of colour from the hibiscus blooms reminded Gabby of crushed silk.

'If there is anything you need, just dial one,' Judy said as she made to leave.

'Thank you, Judy,' Vinn said with an easy smile as he held the door open for her.

The door closed once Judy had left, and Gabby felt a shiver run up her spine when Vinn's grey-blue gaze sought hers.

'How about a swim to cool off?' he asked.

'Um… OK…' She turned to where her bag was, on the luggage rest beside Vinn's, her belly a nest of nerves at the thought of sharing this penthouse with him. It was very spacious, but it was also incredibly secluded.

Not only had she never shared a bed with Tristan, she hadn't even shared a bathroom with him. He had insisted on having his own—the reason for which Gabby hadn't found out until a few months before his death. She had gone in there in search of more soap for her own bathroom and had seen the telltale traces of white powder and the rolled-up twenty-dollar bill lying on the marble benchtop.

It had not been so much of a shock to find out her husband was regularly snorting cocaine. What had been the biggest surprise was how she hadn't until then guessed it. His erratic moods, his almost manic behaviour at times and his lugubriousness at others, she'd realised in retrospect, were all signs of a drug habit slipping out of control. Just like her parents' inability to accept Blair had been struggling with an addiction, Gabby had not wanted to face the fact her husband was a drug-user. Along with his numerous affairs it had remained yet another dirty secret—another lie to live with.

'I will leave you to get changed,' Vinn said from the door. 'I'm going to have a look at the gym set-up.'

Gabby clutched a bikini and sarong against her chest as she looked at him. 'Oh…right… thanks…'

The door closed on his exit, and she let out a breath that rattled all the way past her lips.

The beach outside their apartment was about two hundred metres long, before an outcrop of rocks cut it off from the next bit of shore. Gabby swam back and forth in a leisurely fashion, enjoying the feel of the water against her skin. When she opened her eyes underwater she could see thousands of colourful tropical fish darting about beneath her. The sandy bottom made the water as clear as glass, and even when she swam out further to sea the clarity was unaffected.

She was quite far out from the shore when a dark shape appeared, seemingly out of nowhere. She gave a startled gasp, her heart pounding like a jackhammer, but then she realised it was Vinn.

'You really shouldn't come out this far without someone with you,' he said, treading water in front of her. 'It could be dangerous.'

'I'm a strong swimmer,' she said, trying not to look at the water droplets clinging to his dark lashes, making them thick and spiky.

'Strength and fitness have very little to do with safety when it comes to getting cramp or being stung by a jellyfish,' he pointed out.

'You don't seem to find it a problem, being out of your depth,' she returned with spirited defiance.

He came up closer, every now and again one of his long legs brushing against hers beneath the water. 'That's because it's rare for me to be out of my depth.' His grey-blue eyes dropped to her mouth as he added, 'In any situation.'

Gabby's tongue flicked over her lips, tasting salt, and her own need clawed at her from inside with long-taloned fingers. He was too close, but she hadn't moved away—even though she had the width of the beach to do so. The brush of his thighs stirred her blood, making it rush through her veins at breakneck speed.

When his head came down she had already lifted her face to meet his, and their lips came together in a hardened press that contained the potency of frustration, urgency and deep-seated passion.

Gabby whimpered with delight when his tongue found hers, tangling with it, seducing it, and then ruthlessly subduing it. She faintly registered she was no longer keeping herself afloat; his arms were wrapped around her, holding her so close their near-naked bodies were almost as one. She felt his erection pressing with such strength and power against her that the breath was pushed right out of her lungs. Desire licked through her, long-tongued and feverish, making every nerve in her body zing with sexual energy.

Vinn lifted his mouth from hers. 'You don't know how close I am to thrusting myself into you right here and now,' he said, in a tone gravel-rough with need.

Her caramel-brown eyes flared in excitement—the same excitement he could feel in every delicious curve of her body pressed so tightly against him. She sent her tongue out to her lips, driving him wild with longing, and her smooth legs tangled with his.

'Do you think that's such a good idea, out here in the open?' she asked in a breathless voice. 'Someone might see us.'

'Right now I couldn't care less who sees us,' he said. 'But for the sake of decency perhaps we should take this indoors.'

She shivered in his arms, but not from cold.

She felt warm and vibrant, and pliable with desire. It was immensely satisfying for him to feel that from her, even if so far it had only been physical, not verbal. She wanted him as much as he wanted her. And, God, did he want her. Every throbbing part of him was aching to sink into her, to feel surrounded by her honeyed flesh. He had dreamed of it for years, hating himself for his weakness where she was concerned, but knowing he would never be truly satisfied until he had taken her. It was a fever in his blood; it ran like a turbulent flood beneath his skin, a pounding river of need, desperate to burst from its confines.

He led her out of the water, his eyes drinking in the sight of her clad only in a red string bikini. Her slim limbs were golden and smooth, her beautiful breasts protesting about the tiny triangles keeping them in place, and the shadow of her cleavage making his imagination run riot.

There were so many things he wanted to do to her, he thought as he took her hand and led her towards the penthouse apartment. He wanted to kiss every secret place, brand her as his in every position possible, so she would no longer think of anyone but him when they made love. He wanted to pump himself into her, to make her swell with his seed, to stake his claim on her in the most primal way of all—as the father of her children. She would think twice about walking away from him if they shared the bond of a child—a child he would love with his whole being, sacrificing everything for it, just as his mother had done for him.

The penthouse was blessedly cool after the heat down on the beach, but Gabby still felt as if she was on fire. As Vinn closed the door she stood before him, trembling all over with anticipation. He had stoked her desire to an unbearable level. She could no more say no to him now than walk on the water they had just left. It was an inevitable outcome of their union—something they had both wanted for longer than perhaps she was prepared to acknowledge. And his longing was more than obvious.

It might not be dressed up in pretty words, such as those said to her by Tristan Glendenning to get her to marry him, but somehow Gabby suspected Vinn Venadicci was not going to be the disappointment in bed her late husband had been.

Sexual potency practically oozed from Vinn's olive-toned pores. He had no doubt bedded many women, done things to them she had never even thought of, and yet he was here with her now, tied to her, aroused by her and reaching for her.

Her bikini top was the first thing to go. Her breasts fell free, the achingly tight nipples soon soothed by the hot, moist cavern of his mouth. It was mind-blowing to feel the rough abrasion of his jaw on her tender flesh. And it was knee-buckling to feel him reach for the strings that held her bikini bottoms in place. They fell to the floor in a silent puddle of red fabric, her body totally exposed to him in a way it had never been before.

'You are beautiful,' he said, in that same roughened tone he had used down on the beach. His gaze ran over her. 'So stunningly beautiful.'

Gabby felt her breath hitch as his eyes came back to hers. 'I want to see you too.' *Was that what she had just said?* she wondered in amazement. Had she openly admitted how much she wanted him?

He held his arms up, as if in surrender. 'I'm all yours,' he said. 'I'll give you the honours.'

Gabby needed no other inducement. She reached out with fingers not quite steady and peeled back the black Lycra covering him, her throat almost closing over as she saw how he was made. He was big, far bigger than she had expected, even though she had been pressed up against him so intimately several times. He was as nature intended him—fully male and fully aroused.

Her fingers skated over him, like a light-footed dancer going through a complicated routine, taking her time, rehearsing, going back over the same part again and again to get it right.

'God, that feels so good,' he said, as he captured her hand and held it aloft. 'But I don't want to arrive ahead of schedule.'

Gabby felt her belly quiver like a not-quite-set jelly. She was not used to this extended routine. This strung-out torture of the senses, the screaming of desires begging to be fulfilled. Her body ached for him as it had never ached before. Silky fluid moistened her intimately, swelling her feminine folds with longing. Her breasts were tight and tender at the same time, and her mouth was already missing the heat and fiery conquering of his.

So she did what any aroused woman would do under the circumstances. She pressed herself up against him, her mouth taking his in a hot, wet kiss that showed him how much she wanted him.

He responded just the way she'd wanted him to. He pressed her to the bed behind her, his weight coming over her, his body piercing her in one thick urgent thrust that should not have hurt but somehow did.

Vinn felt her flinch and stilled his movements, raising himself up on his arms to look down at her. 'Am I going too fast for you?'

She gave her head a little shake. 'No…it's just been…a long time…'

Vinn hated being reminded of who had taken her first. It made his blood almost singe his veins to think of that silver-tongued creep having her night after night, pleasuring her the way *he* wanted to pleasure her. He would make her forget him. He would do everything in his power to make her forget, to have her scream his name when he took her to paradise.

'I'll slow down,' he said, pressing a soft kiss to her bow of her mouth. 'Relax for me, *cara*, go with me, don't tense up.'

He moved slowly, relishing the tight warmth of her, but still conscious of her hesitancy. He could feel it—the way her muscles locked as if she was frightened he would hurt her.

'That's it,' he soothed as she started to pick up his slow but steady rhythm. 'You're doing great, Gabriella, just great. Come with me, nice and slow.'

Gabby started to feel the slow melt of her bones. He was so gentle, and yet so powerful.

She could feel the latent strength of him sliding inside her, each slow thrust going a little bit deeper. She felt the tremors begin, but they were not enough to satisfy the ache she felt so deep inside. She writhed beneath him, desperately seeking what she was looking for—something extra, something that would tip her over the edge of oblivion and make her his for all time.

He moved his hand down between their tightly locked bodies, searching for the tight pearl where all her need seemed to be concentrated, and began a gentle but rhythmic stroking. Sensation after sensation flowed through her. She felt herself climbing a steep cliff; she was almost there, the plunge over the edge was so close she could almost taste it, but she kept pulling back, too frightened to finally let go.

'Come for me, *cara*,' Vinn said, kissing her mouth into soft malleability. 'Don't hold back. Let yourself go.'

She concentrated, trying so hard to keep those other dark images out of her mind, her breathing coming in quick sharp bursts. 'I can't...' she gasped, almost close to tears, annoyed at herself for being such a failure. 'I'm sorry... I just can't...'

He slowed his movements, giving her a break from the caressing of his fingers as if he sensed how fragile she felt. 'It's all right,' he said softly. 'We don't have to rush this. Take your time. I can hold on. Only just, mind you, but I can hold on.'

Gabby looked at him with shame colouring her cheeks. 'I can't do this...' she said. 'I've never been able to do this...'

A frown pulled at his brow, and she felt his whole body tense above and within hers. 'What are you saying, Gabriella?' he asked in a raspy tone.

Gabby pressed her lips together, hoping she wouldn't dissolve into tears, but still perilously close all the same.

'Are you saying you have *never* had an orgasm?' he asked after a moment.

She gave a small nod, silent tears making their way down her cheeks.

Vinn recalled her hesitancy, the flinching as if

she had expected him to be rough with her. His heart began to pump—hard, out-of-rhythm pumps against his breastbone—as dark thoughts assembled themselves in his head.

His one short sharp curse cut through the air like a switchblade. 'Did that bastard hurt you?' he asked.

She didn't answer, but he saw all he needed to know in the wounded caramel-brown of her eyes, in the way her bottom lip trembled ever so slightly. His gut clenched, tight fists of anguish punching at his insides, making him see red dots of rage behind his eyes.

He moved away from her as gently as he could. 'I'm sorry, Gabriella,' he said huskily. 'I would never have taken things this far and this soon if I had known.'

She reached out a soft hand and touched him on the arm. 'It's all right, Vinn,' she said. 'I want to know what it's like. I want you to pleasure me. I was so close… I'm sure I can do it…with you…'

Vinn wavered for a moment. His mind was all

over the place. She had been married for five years and apparently not once experienced the ultimate pleasure of physical union. What was he to make of that? He'd already suspected she hadn't loved Glendenning, but she had responded to *him* without restraint. He didn't want to think too much about that. He wasn't prepared to examine his own feelings, much less hers.

'I don't want to hurt you,' he found himself saying, even as his body sought the silky warmth of hers, sliding back in with a shiver of goosebumps lifting the entire surface of his skin as he felt her accept him smoothly. 'Tell me how fast, how slow, what you need.'

She gripped his buttocks tightly in her hands. 'I just need you,' she said. 'No one has ever made me feel like this before.'

She gave a breathy sigh as he began to move, slowly building up the tempo, caressing her, testing how much or how little she needed, gauging her reaction by feeling the pulse of her body and watching the flitting emotions on her face.

He knew when she was coming close. He could feel it in her body, wrapped so tightly around his, and he could see it in the contortion of her features, in the agony and the ecstasy played out on her face. He felt the first ripple course through her, heard her startled cry, and then the aftershocks as wave after wave consumed her, tossing her about in his arms, triggering his own response with a force that was beyond anything he had ever experienced. He felt himself spill, and that delicious moment or two of nothing but intense pleasure. Shockwaves reverberated through him, inducing a lassitude that made him slump over her almost helplessly, like a bit of flotsam tossed up by a very rough surf to the sandy shore.

When he finally had the energy to lift himself above her, Vinn saw that she was crying. Not noisy sobs, just silent tears that tore at him like nothing else could.

He brushed the hair back from her face, his thumb lingering over the soft swell of her bottom lip that her perfect white teeth seemed so deter-mined to savage. 'You were amazing,' he said. 'Truly amazing.'

Her eyes couldn't quite make the full distance to his. 'I didn't realise how…how intense it could be…'

He pressed a soft kiss to her brow. 'It gets better when you know what your body needs. I am still learning about yours—how it responds, what it wants, what it doesn't like, how soft, how hard, that sort of thing.'

She looked at him with an open vulnerability he had never seen in her gaze before—or at least not to that extent. 'Did I pleasure you?'

He frowned as he saw the deep-seated inse-curity in her gaze. 'How can you doubt it, *cara*?'

She began to finger the scar that slashed his left eyebrow in two. 'I've always felt such a failure… physically,' she said, her voice so soft he had to strain his ears to hear it. 'Tristan never touched me during our engagement…apart from kissing and holding hands. He told me he wanted to wait until we were married…' She took a deep breath and added, 'I didn't realise he was having affairs. They went on for most of our marriage.'

Vinn frowned as he absorbed the information. Somehow he had thought Gabriella had turned a blind eye to Glendenning's affairs for the sake of the prestige of being his wife. Had he got it wrong?

'When did you find out about it?' he asked.

Her eyes moved out of reach of his. 'Just after our wedding. I found him in a rather…er…compromising situation.'

His gut tightened. 'How compromising?'

Her cheeks were cherry-red, her voice unsteady, and still her eyes would not meet his. 'He was being…' She winced as if she didn't like using the word. 'Serviced by his secretary…'

Vinn let out another curse as he got off the bed. He whipped a towel around his waist and began to pace. 'For God's sake, Gabriella, why the hell didn't you tell anyone? The marriage could have been annulled. Even then it wouldn't have been too late.'

She swallowed tightly, her eyes glistening with tears. 'My parents had been through so much,' she said. 'I didn't want to cause another scandal. I could just imagine the scene. Mum was so proud of the wedding—how she had dragged herself out of her depression and come off the tranquilisers. How could I do that to her? They had already been through so much. I just couldn't do it.'

Vinn frowned. 'I swear to God if I had been there I would have stopped it. But you made sure I wasn't there, didn't you?'

She bit her lip. 'I didn't want a scene, Vinn,' she said. 'I didn't want Mum and Dad upset.'

His top lip curled. 'Didn't your husband tell you he was the one who gave me this?' He pointed to the slash of the scar on his eyebrow.

She went white, her mouth dropping open. 'No... *No...*'

'He got his thugs to hold me down—all three

of them,' he said, bitterness heavy in his tone. 'And then he shoved the heel of his shoe on my face, telling me it was a gift from you.'

CHAPTER NINE

GABBY thought she was going to faint. In fact she felt as if the vicious assault Vinn had just described had hit *her* full in the face.

She flinched away, her shocked gasp tearing at the dry ache in her throat. She couldn't speak, no matter how hard she tried; the words were stuck behind that boulder-sized restriction in her throat. Vinn had been brutally assaulted, and for all this time he had thought *she* had orchestrated it. Yes, she had spoken to her father's security head Tony Malvern on the phone, asking him to not admit Vinn Venadicci into the church the following day. But she had not told him to use any sort of violence. Besides, Tony was not that sort of man. He was a loving husband and father—a bit tough on the outside, but never would she believe him capable of being party to such a cowardly and vicious attack on another person. All Gabby had done was to tell him to inform Vinn he wasn't welcome to attend the ceremony in case he took it upon himself to disrupt it, as he had threatened.

'N-no… *No!*' Gabby cried. 'I didn't ask anyone to hurt you! You have to believe me, Vinn. Why would I do such a thing?'

His eyes were diamond-hard, the cast to his features as if carved from granite. 'You resented me from the moment I walked through the gates of your family estate. You looked down your nose at me with increasing disdain as the years went on. Don't you remember how much you enjoyed taunting me, Gabriella? Setting me up just so you could giggle behind the bushes with your empty-headed friends?'

Gabby could feel her shame in the slow burn of her cheeks. 'I know I was a bitch towards you,' she said. 'I've explained it already…how I was jealous of you cutting in on my relationship with Blair. He had no time for me whenever you were around.'

'You didn't seem to mind his relationship with other people,' he commented. 'Your late husband being a case in point.'

'That was different,' she said. 'Blair and Tristan had been at school together. Also, Tristan was my mother's best friend's son. He had been coming to our house even before I was born. I was used to sharing my brother with him. It was all I knew.'

His eyes were still trained on hers—hard, un-reachable, and unrelentingly angry. 'Do you deny you asked Glendenning to keep me away from the wedding?' he asked.

Gabby compressed her lips, releasing them after a moment. 'Of course I deny it. I admit I spoke to Tony Malvern, my father's chief of security, but only to ask him to refuse you entry to the church. But I never said a word to Tristan about it.'

Vinn studied her for several tense moments,

weighing up whether or not to believe her. Although Tony Malvern no longer worked for Henry St Clair, since taking early retirement due to a chronic health condition, Vinn had never found him to be anything other than a hardworking and decent family man, who was paid to keep an eye on the various St Clair's business properties after hours.

'Did anyone overhear your conversation with Tony?' he asked.

She gave him a flustered look. 'I don't know… I was upset. I wasn't looking around corners to see if anyone was listening.'

'No doubt your husband was.'

Her frown deepened. 'You went out drinking,' she said. 'That's what I was told when I got back from my honeymoon. They told me you got drunk, and then got into some sort of brawl and ended up in hospital. But if you were assaulted as you said by those thugs, including Tristan, why didn't you press charges?'

'And drag your parents through a very public

scandal, with their beloved daughter at the centre of it?' he asked with a sardonic lift of one brow. 'I might be a bit rough for your tastes, Gabriella, but I am not without feeling or a sense of honour.'

Gabby dropped her shoulders, her thoughts in turmoil. He had hated her for all these years for what she had supposedly done, and yet he had protected her family and therefore her as well. He had not once spoken of it to her parents, of that she was sure. Instead his anger towards her had quietly simmered in the background, as he'd waited patiently for the chance to have his revenge. By going to him for financial help that day she had unwittingly handed him one on a platter.

She brought her gaze back to his hardened one. 'That's what this marriage you've forced on me is all about, isn't it?' she said. 'You wanted to make me pay for the attack you think I ordered by locking me into a loveless marriage with you?'

His expression was unapologetic. 'I told you my reasons for wanting this marriage to take place,' he said in a gritty tone.

'Oh, yes,' she threw at him resentfully. 'You've been lusting after me for years and you just couldn't wait to get your hands on me.'

His eyes burned into hers, with a satirical glint lighting them from behind. 'I didn't hear you saying no just a little while ago,' he said. 'In fact I seem to recall you *begging* me to make love to you.'

Gabby swung away from him in fury, unable to bear his mockery of her desperate need of him. As angry as she was, she still felt the thrumming pulse of blood in her veins, the heady awareness of him and how he had made her feel. Her body was still damp from him. If it wasn't for the fact she was on the pill to regulate her cycle she might have even conceived the child he had bought and paid her to bear for him.

The thought of her belly ripe with his seed made her knees weaken unexpectedly. He might not have married her for the right reasons, but she had no doubt he would make a wonderful father. He had loved his mother more than any other son she had ever known, putting his own life on hold to nurse her through the last months of her too-short and too-hard life.

'Nothing to say, Gabriella?' he asked. 'No feisty comeback to insult me or put me in my place?'

Gabby let out a rattling breath and faced him. 'I'm sorry, Vinn, for what happened to you that night,' she said, taking her pride in hand. 'I know you don't believe me…might never believe me…but I had nothing to do with it. Tristan may have overheard my conversation with Tony, but even if he didn't he had good enough reason to stop you from coming to the wedding.'

'What was that?' he asked, holding her gaze with steely intent.

Gabby chewed at her lip, her eyes falling away from his. 'I'm not sure if he saw us kissing that night… I've often wondered…'

'He was jealous that you responded to me in a way he could never get you to respond to him,' he said. 'I don't blame him. I have revisited that kiss a thousand times in my head, and no one has come close to making me feel the way I did with your mouth on mine.'

Gabby felt warmth flow through her at his words. It was like warmed honey flowing through her veins. He had revisited that kiss so many times—as she had done over the years. What would he say if she were to tell him how often she had thought of how she had responded to him that night? How alive her senses had been, as if he had flicked a switch on in her body no one else had access to?

She had been attracted to him for so long but had stoically denied it.

She had always been in love with him, but too terrified to admit it.

Once the admission was out, Gabby felt it rush through her like the cleansing tide of saline in grit-filled eyes.

She was in love with him.

She had felt that tug of attraction from the moment her female hormones had switched on in her youthful body. She had somehow recognised him as her match, the one person who could meet her needs, but she had pushed him away out of fear, out of insecurity, and out of misplaced pride.

Would her parents have really objected if she had told them all those years ago she loved Vinn instead of Tristan? They had lately accepted the news of her hasty marriage to Vinn without a ripple of disapproval. Even her mother, who had been so toffee-nosed towards him and his mother in the past, had practically wept as she had welcomed him into the bosom of the St Clair family…or what was left of it, Gabby thought with a painful ache, as a vision of her brother flitted into her brain.

Blair had adored Vinn. They had been mates from the word go—comrades, confidantes, all the things good friends should be.

And yet Blair had ended his life…

While his best friend was several thousand kilometres away, nursing his mother on her deathbed, Gabby realised with a stun-gun jolt of awareness.

'Is something wrong?' Vinn's voice sliced through her reverie. 'You look pale.'

'I'm fine…' she said, mentally shaking her head to get her thoughts into some sort of order. 'I'm just thinking…trying to make sense of it all…'

'What happened back then doesn't have to affect us now,' he said. 'If you say you had nothing to do with the assault, then I will have to accept that.'

She looked at him again, swallowing against the lump of uncertainty in her throat. 'How can you ever know for sure I wasn't behind it? You don't trust me; you have no reason to trust me.'

He leaned back against the wall, his arms folded across his broad chest, his eyes still holding hers. 'As long as I am certain you were not party to it, I will be happy,' he said. 'I would not like our future children to think that at one point their mother was intent on bringing about my demise.'

Gabby felt her knees give another distinctive wobble. 'You seem in rather a hurry to land yourself an heir,' she said. 'What if I prove to be infertile?'

'Have you any reason to suspect you might be?'

'Have you any intention of releasing me from this arrangement if I am?' she countered.

His grey-blue eyes tussled with hers, bringing hers down in a submission she resented but couldn't for the life of her control. 'No,' he said. 'If you can't give me an heir naturally, then we will pursue the other options available.'

'What if I don't want to have a child right now?' Gabby asked, and then, after a carefully timed interval, added, 'What if I don't want to have children at all?'

The silence that ensued grew teeth that seemed to gnaw at the space that separated them.

'Do you have a particular aversion to motherhood?' he finally asked.

'Not really...' She waited a moment before continuing, 'I guess what I have an aversion to is being forced to deliver according to someone else's schedule, not mine.'

'Having a child should ideally be a joint decision,' he said, still honing in on her with those unreadable grey-blue eyes of his. 'If you are not ready, then we will wait until you are.'

'You don't even like me,' she said, frowning at him in irritation. 'How can you possibly think of fathering a child with me?'

His eyes ran over her sheet-wrapped form in one sweeping, all-encompassing movement that had possession and arrogant control written all over it. 'Because I have always wanted you, Gabriella,' he said. 'You are my nemesis, my other half, my completion. It was confirmed when we came together physically. I always knew it would be like that between us. I just had to wait until you were willing to see it.'

Gabby felt the need to keep some level of distance. 'What if Tristan hadn't died?' she asked. 'Would you have continued with this vendetta?'

He raised one broad shoulder in shrug. 'That would have entirely depended on you,' he said. 'I was testing the waters the night before your wedding. I was convinced you were no more in love with Glendenning than he was with you, and it seems I was right. No woman in love with another man would have responded the way you did to me.'

'So…kissing me was some sort of experiment?' Gabby asked, with reproach heavy in her tone.

'Kissing you was a temptation I could not resist,' he responded, stepping towards her, holding her in place with his hands on the tops of her shoulders. 'Like it is now, *cara*. I want to feel the tremble of your lips beneath mine, the way your tongue so shyly meets mine. I want it all, Gabriella. I want all of you.'

Gabby would have pushed him away, but he had already brought her too close to the tempting heat of his near-naked body. With only a towel loosely slung about his hips, she was left in no doubt of his arousal. Her body was just as eager behind its flimsy shroud of a sheet. Her nipples were clearly outlined, pert and aching for his touch, and her body was swaying towards him.

Her mouth opened just as his was lowering to commandeer hers.

The kiss was like two combustible fuels meeting. Explosions went off in her brain, sending a fiery trail through her veins, making every nerve stand to attention. Her tongue snaked out to meet his in a sexy tangle of duelling need. Hers was igniting slowly but surely; his was at the ready, urgent, pressing, and totally, intoxicatingly, irresistibly male.

'You know I want you again, don't you?' he murmured against her mouth, as his hands skated so very skilfully over her, removing the sheet as if it was a layer of tissue wrap.

Gabby's hands had already dispensed with his towel, and were now shaping him, relishing in the tilted engorgement of him that so matched her body's intimately designed contours.

'I want you too,' she said, pressing kiss after kiss to his mouth. 'I want to feel it all again. Make me feel it all again.'

Vinn didn't need her to beg or plead. He wanted

it as much as she did—the magic, the mindlessness of it, the total exhilaration of the senses that shoved aside every other rational thought. He didn't want to think just now. He wanted to feel. He had unlocked in her a treasure chest of sensuous pleasures, and he wanted to lay each and every precious piece out for his indulgence. The way she shivered when his hands touched her in the lightest of touches. The way her eyes flared when he looked at her with unwavering desire. The way her mouth softened, as if preparing for the hard descent of his, her lips parting to accept the searching thrust of his tongue.

God, had any woman done this to him in the past? With her he seemed to be always fighting for control, holding back the urge to spill, his need so great he had trouble reining it in to ensure she was not rushed, not hurt the way she had been in the past.

'Vinn?' Her soft voice was against his neck, her lips brushing his flesh.

He stroked the back of her head, his fingers

splayed to feel the silky softness of her hair, to anchor him to her, to keep her where she was—close, so very close, so he could feel every beat of her heart.

'Don't talk, *mia piccola*,' he said, cupping her face to look deep into her eyes. 'Just feel.'

Gabby's eyelashes fluttered closed as his mouth came down to reclaim hers, the intimate contact so consuming she felt her mind spinning out of control. His kisses were so drugging they made her forget the past. They made her think only of the here and now, of how he made her feel, of how her body responded to him, of how it came alive in a way it had never done before. She could feel the echo of his kiss resounding in the rest of her body. It made her aching need for him all the more intense. It throbbed in her belly, low and deep, it swelled in her breasts, making them eager for his touch, and it trembled in her fingertips as she continued to explore him.

His hand pulled hers away from his hardened body, holding it above her head as he ravaged her mouth with his lips and tongue. Gabby laid her head back against the wall as he subjected her to a conflagration of the senses, her heart pounding inside her chest, her legs barely able to keep her upright.

He lifted his mouth off hers long enough to guide her back to the bed, his hands shaping her breasts, his mouth bestowing hot, sucking kisses to each one until she was twisting and turning beneath him as he pinned her with his weight.

'I have thought of doing this to you for so long,' he groaned against her right breast. 'I don't think there is a man alive who has wanted a woman more than I have wanted you.'

Gabby knew his attraction for her was only physical. He had said nothing of other feelings. At least he wasn't lying to her, as Tristan had done, but still she felt achingly disappointed her love for him was not returned. Was she destined to be tied to men who wanted to exploit her? Was she never to feel loved for who and what she was? She longed for security, for the warm protection of a love that would not die in spite of the passage of years. And yet into this loveless arrangement Vinn wanted to bring children—their children—a mingling of their blood and DNA. How could she agree to such a scheme without the assurance that he felt something for her other than lust?

'Vinn?' she said, touching his face with the flat of her palm, her fingers splaying over his stubbly jaw before she could stop them.

He turned his head and pressed a kiss into the centre of her palm. 'Do we have to talk right now, *cara?*' he asked, his eyes heavy-lidded with banked-down desire.

'Do you still hate me?'

His grey-blue eyes opened fully, and then focussed on hers. 'No,' he said on an expelled breath. 'Hate is not what I feel for you.'

Gabby drew in a ragged breath and held it. 'You…you don't?'

His eyes were unwavering on hers. 'I would not be here now, doing this to you, if I hated you, Gabriella,' he said.

'But you don't love me,' she said. And, waiting a beat, added, 'Do you?'

The distance between his brows narrowed slightly. 'That seems to me to be a rather loaded question,' he mused. 'Is that a prerequisite for allowing me access to your body? Showering you with empty words and phrases just so I can have my physical needs met?'

Gabby felt a stirring of resentment at his words. 'I am not entirely disconnected from my feelings, and I don't believe you are either,' she said. 'You make love to me as if you worship every inch of the space I take up, and yet you won't admit a modicum of affection for me. How am I supposed to make sense of it all?'

He eased himself up on his elbows, his weight still pinning her, pelvis to pelvis, stomach to stomach. 'Do you want me to tell you I love you?' he asked. 'Is that it? Is that what you want? For me to pretend to have feelings for you?'

Gabby blinked back tears. 'No, I don't want you to pretend to love me,' she said, trying to keep her voice steady. 'That's not what I want at all.' *I want you to love me for real.*

'Why is what I feel or don't feel suddenly so important to you?' he asked.

She frowned at the harshness of his tone. 'Because almost every woman wants to be assured the man she is involved with is not just using her physically. It's so degrading, so emotionless and…and dehumanising.'

He lifted himself off her, the sudden rush of cooler air on her chest and stomach making her feel not just physically abandoned, but emotionally as well.

She watched as he reached for the towel she had peeled off him just moments ago, wrapping it around himself almost savagely.

Anger flickered in his grey-blue eyes, and his body was whipcord tense as he faced her. 'Is that what you think I am doing?' he asked. 'Slaking my lust with no regard whatsoever for who you are and what you might need? Didn't the last half-hour prove *anything* to you about who I am as a person?'

Gabby pressed her lips together to keep them from trembling. 'You married me to possess me,' she said. 'I am the highly prized trophy you missed out on in the past. You know I would not have married you for any other reason than money, so you swooped as soon as the opportunity arose.'

'I am not denying I have wanted you for a very long time,' he clipped back. 'But don't let's confuse the issue with pretending things we don't feel. You have looked down your nose at me for as long as I can remember. Sure, we just had great sex—better even than I thought it would be—but that doesn't mean either of us has to pretend things we don't feel in order to feel better about the level of desire we just experienced and will no doubt continue to experience.'

Gabby pulled the sheet up to her chin. 'I don't think you would admit to loving someone even if you did,' she said. 'You wouldn't want to let anyone, particularly a woman, get the upper hand—and certainly not me.'

He gave a mocking laugh that chilled her blood. 'Is that what you think? That I've been pining away all these years with unrequited love for you, but I won't admit it in case you get the chance to use it against me in some way?'

Gabby didn't know what to think. She was confused, so very confused, and suddenly feeling more vulnerable than she wanted to be. She was making a fool of herself. She knew it, and it made her feel all the more exposed. She was practically begging him to confess feelings for her he clearly didn't have and never had. She was a fool, a romantic fool, crying for a moon that was never going to rise on her horizon.

She curled up in a tight ball on the bed, dragging the rest of the sheet over her to cover herself. 'I would like to be left alone,' she said in a toneless voice.

Vinn hesitated. He didn't really want to leave her like this, she was upset and very probably close to tears, but he just couldn't stay.

The first heady rush of love he had felt for her

when she was younger had very quickly been replaced by a deep loathing for all she represented. The way she had always carried herself with that cold air of condescension, ridiculing him at every opportunity, had fuelled that hatred to boiling point. But now her adamant denial of having anything to do with his assault had made him rethink everything.

Revenge had been at the forefront of his mind for so long he needed time to re-examine his feelings. Up until a few hours ago she had hated him with an intensity that had glittered in her brown eyes every single time they clashed with his. Yet she had fallen apart in his arms, her body responding to his in a whirlwind of passion. There could be many reasons for that, he thought cynically. Two point four million of them, for starters. Anyway, she hadn't come right out and said it. She had just hinted at having feelings for him. But what if it was his wealth she was really in love with?

OK, he had saved her skin and given her a taste

of what her late husband had denied her. Women were funny like that; one earth-shattering orgasm and suddenly they were madly in love with you. How many times had he heard other women say it to him, only to move on when the first wave of lust died down?

Vinn dragged on his bathers. 'I'm going for another swim,' he said. 'I guess I'll see you later.'

There was a muffled sound from beneath the tightly wrapped sheet that sounded as if she didn't care either way—which was probably no more than he deserved, Vinn thought as he softly shut the door as he left.

CHAPTER TEN

GABBY woke to semi-darkness and to a feeling that someone was in the room with her. She pushed herself upright, brushing the hair out of her eyes as she saw the shadow of Vinn's figure sitting on a chair close to the bed.

'What time is it?' she asked, trying for a cool, calm and collected tone, even though it was far from what she felt.

'Just gone nine.'

'Oh…'

'We can still have dinner in the restaurant, or order in some room service—whichever you prefer,' he said, rising to his feet and stretching.

Gabby wondered how long he had been sitting there, silently watching her. 'I need a shower,' she said. 'Do you think the restaurant will stay open long enough for me to freshen up?'

He switched on the master switch, which activated all the lamps in the suite. 'You are part-owner of this resort, Gabriella,' he reminded her. 'If you want the restaurant to remain open for you, then you only have to issue the command.'

Gabby held the sheet she had gathered around herself up close to her chin. 'Don't mock me, Vinn,' she said. 'Please...not after this afternoon.'

'Is that what you think I'm doing?' he asked, frowning.

She gave him a surly glance. 'Look, I know I haven't got the best business head in the world, but at least I've tried my best to fill the gap my brother left.'

'Is that why you put your hand up for the job?' he asked. 'To fill in for Blair? Even though it was never what you wanted to do?'

Gabby tightened the sheet around her body rather than meet his eyes. 'We do what we do,' she said stiffly. 'There's no turning back.'

'What is that supposed to mean?'

She faced him squarely. 'My parents depend on me, Vinn,' she said. 'Do you think for a moment I would have come of my own volition to see you about the margin call? I only did it for them. I am only here now for them. I am all they have left.'

'So you sacrificed yourself?'

She lifted one shoulder. 'Your words, not mine.'

'But that's how you see it, isn't it?' he asked in an accusing tone. 'You, the Princess, have agreed to marry the peasant to save your family from financial shame.'

Gabby flinched at the weight of bitterness in his tone. 'I don't see you as a peasant, Vinn,' she said. 'I have never thought of you that way.'

His top lip curled. 'Nice try, Blondie. You nearly had me there. You sound so convincing, but we both know you will always see me as the cleaner's son. You married down, sweetheart, *way* down. How does it feel?'

Gabby held his fiery look for a beat or two

before slowly lowering her gaze. 'It certainly feels a whole lot better than my previous marriage,' she said, and then, meeting his eyes once more, added, 'That is unless you are going to add to your repertoire of accusing me of being a bitchy snob with the occasional slap or punch to bring me to heel.'

The silence began to pulse, each drawn out beat increasing the tension to snapping point.

Vinn stared at her, his eyes twin pools of stormy grey and blue. 'You mean to tell me that…he *hit* you?'

She nodded grimly. 'Not all the time, but often enough to keep me terrified he would do it again. It was a power thing. I wasn't the woman he really wanted. His parents would never have accepted any of the women he was having affairs with, so he used me as a punching bag now and again to keep me in line. I soon learned to keep my head down.'

Vinn's stomach churned. His hands felt numb even though he was clenching and unclenching them. 'Why didn't you say something?' he asked. 'For God's sake, Gabriella, you took years of that from him?'

She hugged her arms across her chest. 'I wanted to tell so many times,' she said. 'But I would have hurt people. My parents adored Tristan—he was like a second son to them. He had been so good when Blair died—he'd helped organise the funeral, and he even gave the eulogy.' She released a breathy sigh and continued. 'And then there were his parents—his well-connected parents, with a legal pedigree longer than your arm. Appearances are everything to them. How do you think they would have reacted to a spousal abuse claim against their beloved son lodged by me?'

Vinn swallowed tightly. He could see she had been in an impossible situation. The legal powerhouse the Glendenning family represented would have made anyone think twice about coming forward with such a claim against one of their blue-blooded heirs. She had gone through a living hell, each day a torture of being tied to a man who had treated her appallingly. Glendenning had even used her as a shield, making Vinn believe for all these years she was responsible for the attack on him the night before the wedding.

'I'm sorry,' Vinn said through a throat that felt as if he had swallowed a handful of razorblades. 'I wish I had known what had been going on. I wish you had felt you could have turned to me for help.'

'You were the last person I could turn to, Vinn,' she said, giving him a despondent look. 'You tried to warn me about Tristan and out of stubborn pride I refused to listen. Then, when I realised what a stupid mistake I'd made, I didn't want to hear you say *I told you so*. I just couldn't bear it.'

He scraped one of his hands down his face. 'Everyone is entitled to make a few mistakes in life,' he said. 'God knows I've made plenty. But thanks to the support and direction of people like your father I have been able to turn things around.'

'Some things can never be turned around,' she

said blowing out a sigh. 'After Blair's suicide I felt so guilty… I felt like I had to do something to bring my mother out of her deep depression. My father threw himself into his work, but Mum had nothing…just me. I wanted to give her a new focus—a wedding, grandchildren in the future, that sort of thing. But I didn't stop to examine how I really felt about Tristan, or—even more stupid of me—how he felt about me.'

Vinn took one of her hands and brought it up to his mouth, pressing his lips softly to the back of her knuckles. '*Cara,* don't punish yourself any more,' he said gently. 'You were in no way responsible for your brother's death. He had an addiction problem. He didn't get the help he needed. There was nothing you could have done.'

Vinn's words were like an arrow in Gabby's heart. She would always feel there was something she should have done. That was the pain she had to live with—the regret that she hadn't seen what was right under her nose.

Vinn brushed his lips over her fingers again.

'We all wish many things, Gabriella,' he said. 'Things we would have done differently if we knew then what we know now.'

Gabby felt her breathing start to shorten. 'Does that mean you want to end our marriage?' she asked.

He looked down at her for a long moment. 'Is that what you would like?' he finally asked. 'To be free?'

She couldn't hold his intense gaze, for she was sure he would see the longing and desperation reflected in hers. 'I'm not sure what the press will make of it if we end our marriage on the very day it was formalised,' she said. 'Then, of course, there are my parents to consider.'

'I was thinking the very same thing,' he said in a sombre tone. 'Your father has been through major surgery and is still a long way from being in reliable health. We can hardly fly back to Sydney and announce our separation.'

Gabby brought her eyes back to his, craning her neck to do so. 'So…' she said, moistening her lips with the tip of her tongue. 'What do you suggest we do?'

He gave her another long, studied look. 'I told you the day you came to see me about the margin call that I believed marriage to be a permanent commitment. That has not changed.'

Gabby searched his features, hoping, praying for some clue to how he felt about her. But his expression was unfathomable. She began to toy with the idea of telling him she had fallen in love with him—openly this time, instead of hinting at it as she had done earlier. She even went as far as having the words mentally rehearsed; she could see them inside her head in capital letters: I LOVE YOU.

But something stopped her. He was still coming to terms with all he had learned about her this evening. The dark secret she had kept hidden for so long was finally out, which she could see had not only shocked him but had summoned his pity. She didn't want his pity. She wanted his love and his respect. But it would take more time to secure the latter, and the former she had no control over whatsoever.

All she knew was that he desired her, and had done for as long as she could remember. She had treated his attraction for her with disdain in the past, rejecting him in order to marry a man who had not only exploited her in the worst way possible, but orchestrated a vicious attack on Vinn that had left a lifelong scar—and not just the one on his eyebrow.

Gabby loved Vinn for who he was now just as much as she loved him for who he had been before. He had tried to rescue her from a disastrous marriage. He had done the responsible thing by coming to her as soon as he possibly could and asking her to reconsider. He had even offered himself as a substitute groom to save her pride on the day, and yet she had been too proud to listen.

Gabby thought back to that moment when Vinn's mouth had been sealed to hers. The flames of mutual desire had leapt between their bodies like an out-of-control forest fire, with every sense of hers tuned into his and his into hers, as if they had been programmed from birth to respond to each other in that heady, earth-shattering way.

Had Tristan come up the stairs just at that moment and seen them locked in such a passionate embrace? Or had he been lurking about in the shadows even earlier? Perhaps overhearing the start of Vinn's warning? Not wanting to allow Vinn the chance to besmirch him any further, he had come up in that charming, laid-back way of his and lured Vinn away from the house with a request for a private man-to-man chat that had led to Vinn spending a night in hospital, with no hope of bringing a halt to her marriage from hell?

'Gabriella?' Vinn's voice brought her thoughts back to the present moment. 'You've gone very quiet. Do you not agree we should keep our marriage as it is? For the time being at least?'

Gabby tried to smile, but it contorted her mouth, giving it an unnatural feel. 'I still can't work out why you wanted to marry me in the first place. It seems to me you have paid a heck of a lot of money for a bride who doesn't quite fit the bill of what you were expecting.' She gave him a rueful look. 'You've been short-changed, Vinn, and yet you don't seem to be the least bit annoyed about it.'

This time he took both of her hands in his, squeezing them gently. 'If I am annoyed about anything it is about my own ignorance of your circumstances.'

'It is not your fault,' Gabby said, looking up at him. 'You did the right thing by coming to me, but I was too proud to heed your advice.'

Should she tell Vinn of Tristan's cocaine addiction? Gabby wondered. The thought danced in her mind on tentative feet, like a ballerina on damaged toes, trying to convince the judges at an important audition she was worthy of the role. Every step of the process hurt unbearably, with pain and shame, and also the niggling fear that Gabby might have been partly to blame for Tristan going to such desperate measures. There had been no sign of drug use before their ill-fated marriage, but that didn't mean it hadn't been going on.

'Vinn…' she began. 'Did you know Tristan had a cocaine habit?'

'When did *that* start?' he asked, frowning heavily. 'Before or during your marriage?'

'I'm not sure,' she answered. 'I had never noticed anything untoward before, but then I didn't know he was having affairs either—so who am I to be certain one way or the other?'

'Have you considered Tristan might have been the one to get Blair involved in drugs?' he asked. 'That Tristan was perhaps his supplier?'

Gabby felt her heart slip sideways in her chest. 'Oh no…'

Vinn's expression was grim. 'You were a pawn in his game, *cara*. I am sure of it. He had to use you as a screen to keep things on the level. Especially after Blair died.'

It all made sense now Gabby thought about it. Tristan had intensified his attentions not long after her brother's suicide, insisting on their marriage even though she had been having doubts for months.

'Did you ever consider speaking to my parents the night before the wedding?' she asked.

He closed his eyes for a nanosecond. 'Yes,' he said, scoring a pathway through his hair. 'I did consider it, and I have tortured myself ever since that I didn't seek a private audience with them first. But I guess I felt at the time it was better to start with you, to somehow get you to see the mistake you were making before I approached them. After all, it was your decision. You claimed to be in love with Glendenning, and even though I doubted it I had no way of proving it either way. Other than that kiss.'

That kiss.

The kiss he had revisited so many times, Gabby thought with a delicate flutter of her insides. She looked at his mouth, at the sensual contours of it, the full lower lip her teeth longed to nibble at and her tongue longed to salve with soft moist sweeps and strokes, until he took control in that masterful but spine-loosening, gentle way of his.

His head came down and the kiss became real, exhilaratingly real, as their tongues mated, their lips suddenly hot and wet with mutual need. Gabby pressed herself closer to the turgid heat of his body, her arms going around his waist, then lower. She dug her fingers into the tautness of his buttocks to bring him up against the increasingly urgent pulse of her body.

'It's too soon,' Vinn groaned against her mouth.

'For you?' Gabby asked in mild surprise, nibbling at his lower lip, her lower body rubbing against his rock-hard erection.

'God, no.' He gave a little laugh and nibbled back. 'For you, *cara*. You will be tender inside. You were practically a virgin. You are so small, and I am—'

'So big—and I want you now,' Gabby said with a boldness she had never known she possessed. 'Right now.'

His eyes glittered with need. 'Are you sure?' he asked, stroking the side of her face with one tender hand. 'I can pleasure you instead. There are other ways of releasing the tension without hurting you.'

Gabby felt her heart swell at his concern for her. Didn't that prove he loved her? Why wouldn't he admit it? Did he think she would use it against him? Oh, how much she adored him! Why had she spurned and ridiculed him all those years ago?

'Vinn…' she said, summoning up the courage to tell him how she felt. 'There's something I want to tell you…'

Vinn kissed the side of her mouth, working slowly but steadily towards its throbbing centre. 'You have this rather endearing but no less annoying tendency to want to talk when I want you to feel,' he said. 'What could be more important right now than feeling this…?' He kissed her deeply, and then after a few breathless seconds moved his mouth to the side of her neck, making the sensitive skin there and all over her body lift in a prickly pelt of goosebumps. 'And this…?'

Gabby had no verbal answer. Everything she wanted to say, her body said for her. She squirmed with desire in his arms, desperate to feel his electrifying touch on every part of her. Her breasts swelled with need, her nipples hard as pebbles, aching for the sweep of his tongue or the primal scrape of his teeth to soothe their ache. She pushed herself against him brazenly, throwing her head back, her insides clenching and cramping simultaneously with the anticipation of assuagement.

Vinn's mouth was on her collarbone, his tongue laving a pathway over its fragile scaffold to the sensual flesh of her breasts which he had uncovered. They seemed to swell in his hands, the softness of them like silk and cream, and the tight points of her nipples drew his mouth like a magnet, each stroke of his tongue evoking another sweet gasp of surprise and delight from her lips. She was so keen, and yet he was so hesitant. He didn't want to hurt her. And he *would* hurt her if he drove in without careful regard to her lack of experience.

He eased back, trying to control his breathing, trying to control the thundering roar of the blood in his veins, but her shy fingers searched for him and found him, the work of her fingertips sending arrows of sharp need from his groin to his toes and back, leaving him breathless and out of reach of common sense. He wanted to feel her mouth on him, the wetness and velvet softness of it taking him in, her tongue playing with him, teasing him until he exploded.

He clamped his eyes shut as his dream came alive. She was doing it by the script he had formed in his head. She was shaping him with her hands, discovering his hard length, exploring the detail of it, the moist tip of his need, the stickiness of his essence, banked up and waiting to be summoned by the honeyed grip of her body or the lick or slide of her tongue.

His back arched as he felt her soft, moist mouth

close over him, and the shyness of it was part of the overwhelming allure. She didn't know what she was doing, but she was going on instinct—and everything she was doing was right. His blood surged, his pulse raced, his heart rate soared and his breathing all but stopped as she drew on him, her lips a soft but insistent caress, her tongue a teasing temptress, luring him out of the realms of control into the dark, swirling abyss of release.

Suddenly he was there, the force of it taking him by surprise. He pumped, he spilled, he shuddered—and she accepted it all, not for a moment shrinking away from the rawness of it, not for a second repulsed or shocked by how he had responded to her. Instead she smiled as she came up for air, licking her soft lips as if she had just sampled the elixir of heaven, before pressing a soft kiss to the left of his chest, right where his heart was pounding out of control.

Vinn placed his still shaking hand on the back of her silky head, stroking it absently as his breathing gradually slowed. He couldn't find the words to describe what he was feeling. She had left him stunned, not just physically but emotionally. He had had so many lovers, and not one had moved him as Gabriella had done. And not just then, but before, giving herself to him when she had been so frightened, so terrified he would use her without respect…without love.

Love was a strong word—a word he liked to shy away from, an unfamiliar word to him. Or at least it always had been in the context of sex.

Vinn had loved his mother; he seriously doubted any son could have loved a mother more. And he loved his half-sister—not that he was at liberty to claim her as such. Lily Henderson had sought him out after an exhaustive search, trying to make sense of her place in the world as the love-child of Hugo McCready, a prominent mover and shaker in the corporate world who, even after all this time, obstinately refused to acknowledge the living, breathing harvest of the wild oats he had sowed—Vinn included.

Hugo McCready thought it his worldly privilege to seduce the young housemaids who came to clean up after him, under the nose of his long-suffering wife and three legitimate children. But Vinn suspected that, unlike him, Lily was intent on blowing McCready's cover once and for all. Vinn was primarily concerned that it would hurt her rather than their conscienceless father, and so he had done and would continue to do what he could do to protect her—even if the press consistently misinterpreted their relationship.

Paying off this loan was part of Vinn's plan to outsmart his father and his takeover bid, and it had all gone according to plan—with the added bonus, of course, of securing Gabriella St Clair as his wife. He had denied feeling anything for her but desire, but even while his body ached and throbbed for her there were other feelings he had still to make sense of in his head.

She seemed intent on prying an admission of love out of him, but he still wasn't certain of her motives. Money had a habit of inciting deep feelings in many of the women he had associated with in the past. Why else did women in their twenties marry men old enough to be their grandfathers? The press was full of such cases, where rich old men had adoring, beautiful young women draped on their arms, claiming to love them.

Gabriella St Clair had been used to a certain lifestyle, which she had thought was going to be ripped from beneath her, so she had laid herself at the mercy of the one man she had claimed to dislike intensely for as long as Vinn could remember. For her to suddenly turn around and claim to love him was something Vinn found a little hard to believe, even though they shared a powerful physical chemistry.

But he was starting to realise, irrespective of what she did or didn't feel for him, that perhaps Gabriella had a right to know a little more of his past than she currently did. But telling her about Lily was something he wanted to clear with his half-sister first. Lily was a very sensitive girl of just twenty. Just one year younger than Gabriella had been when she had married Tristan Glendenning. And, like Gabriella, Lily didn't know what she wanted; she was confused and looking for an anchor. Vinn was determined to be that anchor for as long as he needed to be, and to protect her from the unscrupulous man who had fathered her.

Vinn looked down at Gabriella; she was his wife now, in every sense of the word, and his blood surged at the realisation. *She was his wife.* He had made her so, not just in word and at the stroke of a pen, but in the union of their bodies— a union he could still feel buzzing in his veins.

A union he wanted again and again.

CHAPTER ELEVEN

OVER the next few days Gabby was almost able to fool herself her honeymoon with Vinn was as perfect as any other lovestruck bride's could ever be. She felt herself blooming as each lazy sun-filled day passed, with hot, sweaty nights writhing in Vinn's arms, leaving her panting and breathless and even more hopelessly in love. She spent hours watching him, her eyes drinking in every smile he cast her way, her spine melting at every light touch he gave her as they explored the various sheltered coves and beaches and rainforest walks all over the island.

Her body felt so different—so energised and alive. Which she knew had nothing to do with the light golden tan she had developed, or the delicious cuisine she had consumed, which had already gone a long way towards softening the sharp edges of her frame. It was because every nerve was tuned into him, every pore of her skin aware of him, as they lay on secluded beaches on sand as soft as finely ground sugar. He had only to look at her with those smoky grey-blue eyes of his and she would turn to him, opening her mouth for the descent of his, her legs entwining with his hair-roughened ones as he began a sensual exploration of every curve and indentation of her body until her cries of release flew up on the air like those of the wild seabirds around them.

It was the second to last day of their visit to the resort, and Gabby and Vinn had walked to the most remote part of the island, where few of the guests fancied taking a four-hour return journey to access its pristine privacy. Vinn had organised a picnic with the kitchen staff, and had carried a pack with beach towels and extra drinks for the trek back.

After a mouthwatering lunch of tandoori chicken roll-ups and a selection of cheeses and fruit, and a crisp bottle of French champagne, they had made love on the outstretched towels until every part of Gabby's body felt as if it had been refashioned into molten wax. She lay in his arms after the storm of release was over, catching her breath, her eyes closed against the sun, listening to the sound of the gentle lap of water against the shore as Vinn's fingers played idly with her hair.

Their lazy movement gradually stilled, and his breathing was so slow and even she realised he had fallen asleep. She propped herself up on one elbow and looked down at him, her heart swelling inside her chest at how magnificently male he looked, so tanned, so muscular and yet so lean.

She trailed her fingertips over the relaxed curve of his mouth, leaning forward to press a soft-as-a-breeze kiss to his mouth. His lips gave a little shifting movement, as if even in the depths of his slumber he still registered her touch.

She eased herself out of his light hold and wandered down to the water, wading in to thigh depth before slipping under the surface and swimming out at a leisurely pace, enjoying the feel of the salt water on her sun-kissed skin. She had never skinny-dipped until now, and the freedom was totally liberating, not to mention deeply erotic. The water caressed her, making her even more aware of how much pleasure her body could give and receive.

It thrilled her how much Vinn wanted her. He might not claim to love her, but there was every indication he no longer held the angry vengeful feelings of the past. He was tender towards her, protective and considerate of her every need. At first she'd thought he was doing it for show, for the resort staff were often serving drinks by the pool and moving around the grounds, but he acted exactly the same way when they were totally alone. She liked to think he was falling in love with her, but after her mistake with Tristan she didn't trust her judgement.

When Gabby came out of the water a little while later, Vinn was sitting upright on the beach, watching her, his eyes flaring with desire as she walked towards him. She felt a delicious shiver of anticipation run up under her skin as the brush of his gaze set her alight with longing all over again.

'You look like a mermaid, *cara*,' he said as he got to his feet. 'A beautiful mermaid who has risen from the depths of the sea to seduce this mere mortal.'

Gabby's eyes were like twin magnets, drawn to his groin where his erection was already stirring in response to her. Her belly gave a little shuffle-like movement as she came up close—close enough to feel the hard ridge of him pressing against her.

'Some mermaid I must look, without any make-up on and my hair in sandy knots,' she said with a self-effacing grimace.

He smiled and brushed the wet hair back off her face with a gentle hand. 'I don't think I have ever seen you look more exquisite than right now,' he said, placing his hands on the curve of her bottom and drawing her into his heat.

She looked into his eyes and felt her insides turn over. She could feel the pulse of his blood, the thickness of him making her legs turn to water. Her breasts were crushed against his broad chest, the masculine sprinkling of hair there tickling her, tantalising her, and making her nipples tighten.

She drew in a hitching breath as his head came down, the hard urgency of his kiss in perfect tune with hers. Her hands dug into his buttocks to hold him close, her tongue tangling with his, darting and duelling, until she could think of nothing but how much she wanted him to drive deep inside her until she was shuddering and convulsing beneath him.

He pressed her back down on the towels, his mouth moving from hers to attend to each of her breasts, drawing on her until her spine was arched and her body wet and aching for the completion she knew only he could give her.

His first thrust was deep, evoking a gasping cry of delight from between her lips as her body slickly embraced him. He moved with an ever-increasing rhythm, his fingers delving between their rocking bodies to maximise her pleasure. There was no hesitancy about her responses now. Her body responded to him every time with explosive force. It felt as if every part of her shattered into a million tiny pieces for that mindless moment or two when she was tossed in the rolling waves of ecstasy, only coming back to one piece as she felt him finally lose control. She loved the feel of him at his supreme moment—the way he suddenly tensed, the way he sucked in his breath before letting it go, sometimes with a groan, other times with a harsh gasp, or, like now, with a raw, primal-sounding grunt that sent a shower of goosebumps over her skin to think she had made him experience such an intense release.

Gabby stroked her fingers up and down his back, lingering over each knob of his vertebrae, feeling his chest rise and fall against hers, his warm breath dancing against the sensitive skin of her neck.

'That feels nice,' he murmured against the tiny dip near her collarbone.

'I like touching you,' she said, still stroking him.

He propped himself up on his elbow and looked down at her. 'I like touching you too, *cara*,' he said huskily. 'I don't think I will ever get tired of doing so.'

Gabby rolled her lips together and lowered her gaze to his stubbly chin. 'So what happens if some time in the future you do?' she asked, her fingers unconsciously stilling on his back, along with her breath in her chest.

'There will be no divorce, Gabriella,' he said, forcing up her chin so she had to meet his gaze. 'You know the terms.'

She tried to push aside her resentment, but it came flooding back. 'So I suppose if I no longer please you, you'll just hot-foot it to one of your many mistresses and let her see to your needs?'

His grey-blue eyes warred with hers. 'Is that really the sort of man you think I am?' he asked. 'Have you learned nothing about me over the last few days?'

She bit her lip, trying to rein in her emotions.

'I know you like sex, and lots of it,' she said. 'But, as you said before we were married, it is my body you want, that you lust after.'

Vinn eased himself off her and got to his feet. 'Yes, well, things are different now,' he said, turning to dust the sand off his thighs.

Gabby pulled one of the towels around her body. 'How do you mean?'

He turned to look at her, but the angle of the sun made it hard for her to see what was written in his expression. 'You are not the woman I thought you were when I married you,' he said. 'I have had to make certain adjustments since.'

Gabby moistened her mouth. 'Would one of those adjustments be learning to *like* me instead of hating me?'

'I have never hated you,' he said, and then, blowing out a breath, grudgingly admitted, 'Well, maybe I thought I did once or twice in the past, but certainly not now.'

She stayed silent, hope building a rickety scaffold around her thudding heart.

'Gabriella…' He shifted so the shadows were off his face. 'I have always kept my sex-life separate from my emotions. This is the first time I have felt something other than desire for a woman.'

'Are you telling me you…you love me?' she asked in a whisper.

He gave her a teasing smile. 'If love is an almost unbearably tight feeling in your chest every time you see the person you are married to, then, yes, perhaps I am in love with you. Or perhaps I need to see a cardiac surgeon. What do you think?'

Gabby was up on her feet and in his arms, pressing hot, passionate kisses all over his face. 'I think you are the most wonderful person I have ever met,' she said. 'I love you so much. I didn't realise how much until just recently.'

'Enough to get rid of those contraceptive pills you've been taking?' he asked, with a distinct twinkle in his eyes.

Gabby gave him a sheepish look. 'You know about those?'

He kissed her forehead lightly. 'If you need more time, then we will wait,' he said. 'But I would like a family. It is something I have wanted for a long time. I guess growing up as an only child with a single mother has made the yearning all the greater.'

'I will throw my pills away,' she promised. 'I want to bear your children, Vinn. I want to be a wonderful wife for you, to make up for all the awful things I did to you in the past.'

He cradled her against him, resting his chin on the top of her head. 'We are different people now, Gabriella. The past should not dictate our future.'

Gabby tipped her head back to look up at him again. 'Why do you always call me Gabriella?' she asked.

His thumb rolled back and forth over the softest part of her chin, just below her bottom lip. 'It is a beautiful name,' he answered. 'It is also Italian. But if you would like me to call you Gabby then I will try to remember to do so.'

'No.' She smiled. 'I like the way you say my

name. No one says it quite like you do. It sends shivers up my spine—always has.'

'Oh, really? Now, that *is* interesting,' he said with a smile. 'Here I was thinking for all these years you loathed the very sight of me.'

Gabby gave him a twisted smile in return. 'I think it might be true what they say about love and hate being two sides of the same coin,' she said. 'I think I was always so mean to you because I was frightened of the way you made me feel—even as young as I was when you first came to my family's home.'

He cupped her face in his hands. 'Are you still frightened of how I make you feel, *mia piccola?*'

'You make me feel safer than anyone else I know,' she said, gazing up at him devotedly. 'I never thought I would learn to trust another man after Tristan, but in these last few days you have somehow managed to sweep away every single fear I ever experienced.'

His eyes contained dark shadows of regret as they held hers. 'I wish I had been able to protect you from his hands,' he said, his jaw tightening over the words. 'If I had known what was going on I would have had him thrown in jail—but only after I gave him a dose of his own medicine. He only picked on you because he knew you couldn't defend yourself. It's a wonder he didn't...' He visibly flinched. 'God, I don't want to think about what else he could have done to you.'

Gabby pressed one of her palms to his unshaven jaw. 'I don't see myself as a victim any more,' she said. 'I did before, but not now.'

He kissed her softly, almost worshipfully. 'We should head back,' he said as he lifted his mouth from hers. 'We have a long walk ahead, and I don't want you to be too tired for what I have in mind for later tonight.'

Gabby sent him a sultry glance as she reached for her bikini, lying on the sand next to the towels. 'You mean I have to wait until tonight to see what it is?'

He gave her a smouldering look and grabbed her by the waist, bringing her naked body up against his, turning her so his front was to her back, every plane and ridge of his body fuelling her desire like gasoline thrown on a flame.

'Maybe we could reset the timetable just a little,' he said, his teeth starting to nip at her earlobe.

'Fine by me,' Gabby said, on the tail-end of a blissful sigh as his erection probed her from behind.

Was there no end to his mind-blowingly sensual repertoire? He constantly surprised her with what he could do with his hands and mouth and body, and it constantly surprised and shocked her how hers responded. She could feel the pressure building even now, the need so insistent she thought she would die if he didn't plunge into her right there and then. But he made her wait, stringing out the torture until she was almost sobbing for the release she so desperately craved.

'Be patient, *cara,*' he said as he teased her tender, sensitised folds with the erotic promise of penetration. 'You will enjoy it much more if you have to wait for it.'

'I want it now!' Gabby said, pressing herself back into him. 'Don't make me wait any longer.'

He gave a chuckle of laughter and began to probe her—just enough to separate her, but not enough to fill her.

'Tell me what you want, Gabriella,' he growled close to her ear. 'Tell me what you want me to do to you.'

'You know what I want you to do,' she gasped, rubbing up against him wantonly.

'Do you want me to do this?' he asked, and slid inside her in one thick, slow thrust that lifted every hair on her scalp.

'Oh, God, *yes...*' She clutched blindly at his thighs, trying to keep her legs from collapsing beneath her.

'And this?' He began to move inside her, deep and far too slowly.

Gabby felt every nerve ending scream for more friction, more speed, more depth and more urgency. 'Yes...*yes...*' she let out, on a panting breath of rampant need.

He held her hips and drove deeply, gradually increasing the pace until she felt her tension building to the point of no return. She fell over the edge, freefalling into an abyss of cascading sensations, the ripples and contractions of her body sending her into a tailspin of feeling that went on and on and on.

Finally it was over, and the aftershocks like tiny rumbles deep down in her body, but then it was Vinn's turn. Gabby felt every carnal second of it—the way his legs braced themselves for the final plunge, the way his breath sucked in deep in his chest, and the way he suddenly pitched forward, the pumping motion of his body filling her, delighting her, making her feel a feminine power she had never felt before as he spilled the essence of himself into the warm cocoon of her body.

Vinn held her in place, trying to get his breathing to settle, but it was difficult. She had the amazing ability to totally unhinge him, to shatter every sense of control he had fooled himself he still possessed. He had put himself out on a limb, an unusual and totally uncharacteristic position for him, but there it was. He loved her as—he had always done.

He had been fooling himself for years that he felt otherwise, but the truth was he had always wanted only her, had only ever loved her. She was the other half he had been searching for all his life. The trouble was he had found it too early, frightening her off with his single-mindedness, virtually pitching her headlong into another man's arms because she had been scared by the intensity of what he had so clumsily communicated to her.

Vinn cupped her breasts, still reluctant to release her, his body relaxed now, but still encased in hers.

'Do you think you could find your way back in the dark?' he asked. 'You know this island better than I do.'

She slowly turned in his arms and linked her arms around his neck. 'Would it matter if we stayed out here all night?' she asked. 'I don't want this magic moment between us to end.'

He gave her a wistful smile. 'We have to fly home tomorrow, *cara,*' he reminded her. 'Back to the real world.'

'I guess… But I don't want anything to change,' she said. 'I want to be the best wife in the world for you. I don't want to disappoint you.'

He smiled and hugged her close. 'You will not disappoint me, Gabriella,' he said. 'Of that I am sure.'

CHAPTER TWELVE

GABBY sat beside Vinn on the flight back to Sydney, her hand linked with his, her head resting against his shoulder. But her heart was still back on the island.

She had almost cried as she had packed her bag. She had wanted the magic of their honeymoon to go on and on. The blissful sense of security had settled about her shoulders like a shawl, but ever since they had got on the plane it felt as if someone had ripped it away from her, leaving her shivering in uncertainty.

Vinn was mostly silent on the journey back. He kept fidgeting with his watch, as if it was the most fascinating thing in the world, when only hours earlier Gabby's body had been his entire focus.

'Are you OK?' she asked at one point.

He turned to look at her, his expression shuttered. 'Sorry, Gabriella, did you say something?'

'I said, are you OK?' Gabby squeezed his hand but after second or two he pulled out of her hold and reached for the in-flight magazine instead.

'I'm fine,' he said, flipping a few pages, his brow furrowing.

'Have I done something wrong?' she asked after another pause.

He gave her a quick on-off smile. 'No, of course not, *cara*,' he said, patting her hand. 'I have a lot on my mind right now. Business doesn't take a holiday, I'm afraid.'

Gabby felt a twinge of remorse that she hadn't once asked him about his work. She knew so little of what he did, other than he had first made a fortune on a development project in an outlying suburb which had suddenly taken off after a change of council zoning. He had reinvested the profit into more developments, astutely keeping one step ahead of the market so he could maximise his profits.

'Is there anything I can do to help?' she asked.

He shook his head and briefly touched her nearest cheek with his fingertips. 'No, Gabriella. I want you to concentrate on producing me an heir,' he said. 'Your parents need you too, right now. Your father is doing well, but seeing you happy and contented will aid his progress like nothing else can. And a grandchild will be something wonderful for both of them to look forward to.'

Gabby settled back in her seat, smiling to herself as she thought of how she had flushed every one of her contraceptive pills down the sink at the resort apartment. Her hands crept to the flat plane of her belly, wondering what it would feel like to have Vinn's child growing there. Even though she knew it was probably unlikely, since she had only just ceased her protection, she wondered if she was already pregnant. She had been on a low-dose pill, more for convenience than contraception, and the failure rate was a lot higher than other brands…

She reached for his hand again, stroking her fingers up and down his long fingers. 'Thank you, darling, for everything you did to make the last week so special for me,' she said. 'It was a perfect honeymoon.'

He covered her hand with his and gave her another smile, but Gabby couldn't help feeling it looked forced this time. 'It was my pleasure, *cara*,' he said.

'I love you,' she said, stretching across to press her mouth against his.

'I know you do,' he said, still with that not-quite smile.

Gabby started to feel the stealthy creep of doubt; like ghostly fingers tickling the fine hairs on the back of her neck. Why, when she told him how much she loved him, did he not say he loved her too? In fact, when she backtracked through their loving exchange the afternoon before on the beach, she couldn't remember him saying he loved her at all. He had hinted at it, but not openly spoken of his feelings. But then he hadn't had to, she reminded herself ruefully. She had raced in headlong and confessed her love for him, then recklessly thrown away her pills, promising him the heir he so dearly wanted.

But what if that was all he wanted from her? What if, when she gave him the child or children he desired, he decided he no longer had a need for her in his life? He kept saying there would be no divorce, but that didn't mean he wouldn't change his mind some time in the future. After all, he had insisted she sign a pre-nuptial agreement. Didn't that suggest he had no plans or indeed no confidence that the marriage would continue indefinitely?

Everything had happened so quickly. Her father's heart attack, the takeover bid, and the sudden margin call had sent her into a tailspin, tossing her into Vinn's orbit where, two weeks later, she was still spinning.

Gabby didn't get much of a chance to speak with Vinn in private again, for as soon as they got off the plane a driver was waiting to collect them.

They called in to the hospital to see her father briefly, and then Vinn instructed the driver to drop him off at his office, before telling him to take Gabby to his house in Mosman.

Vinn gave her a brief, impersonal kiss before he got out of the car, and within moments he was striding away, his mobile phone already up to his ear.

Gabby sat back with a sigh as the driver nudged back out into the traffic. She had secretly hoped Vinn would do all the traditional things, like carry her over the threshold—perhaps carry her all the way upstairs and make love to her in the bed they would share as man and wife. But he was back to business as if the last seven days hadn't happened. He hadn't even given her a second glance as he had walked through the doors of his office block.

Gabby busied herself with unpacking once the driver had left, after carrying in the luggage for her. She put on a load of washing and while it was running wandered outside to look around the garden. The lawn had been recently mown, but there was no sign of a gardener about the place, for which she was grateful. She needed time to settle into Vinn's house without the speculative gaze of his household staff.

Vinn had arranged the delivery of her car and her clothes on the day of their wedding. All of her things were neatly hung or folded in the walk-in wardrobe off the master bedroom—she assumed by Vinn's house-keeper, although there was no sign of anyone having been in the house for the last few days. The house was clean and tidy, certainly, but there was no fresh food in the refrigerator, so Gabby decided to drive up to the closest shops for some basic supplies.

When Gabby got back to the house Vinn was on the harbourside deck leading off the lounge, his back towards her as he spoke into his mobile phone. The hushed urgency of his tone was what made her step closer on silent feet, and her heart came to a skidding halt in her chest when she heard his words, carrying on the still afternoon air.

'No, *cara*,' he said. 'Trust me. This is not the right time to announce to the world our true relationship.'

Gabby felt as if a knife had been plunged between her ribs, but somehow she remained upright, coldly, determinedly upright, as she listened to the rest.

'I know,' he said, blowing out a sigh. 'I love you too, and I want the world to know how much you mean to me, but do you know what the press will make of this? It's too dangerous. I have a lot in the pipeline—this takeover bid for one thing. I don't want anything to jeopardise that until it is totally secure, which won't be until the end of next week at the earliest.'

There was a pause as he listened to whoever was on the other end, and Gabby's heart thudded painfully as each second passed, in case he turned and saw her standing there, listening to every damning word.

'Look, *cara*,' Vinn went on, raking a hand through his rumpled hair, 'I spent a lot of money on securing this deal. I don't want anything to compromise it at this stage. We have to tread carefully. There are other people to consider in all of this.'

Another pause as he listened to the other person.

'I will have to tell her at some stage,' he said. 'She has a right to know. She is my wife now. But let's leave it a week or two longer, hmm? Just keep your head down, and I will send you some money to tide you over. *Ciao*.'

Vinn closed his phone and turned—to come face to face with the shell-white face of Gabriella.

'*Cara,*' he began. 'I didn't hear you come in.'

Gabby clenched her hands into fists. 'Don't you "*cara*" me, you two-timing bastard,' she bit out in blistering fury.

He took a step towards her. 'Gabriella, you don't understand. I was—'

'Oh, I know what you were doing,' Gabby shot back. 'You were talking to *her*, weren't you?

Your mistress—your mystery lover. The woman you love. I heard you say it.'

'You have misinterpreted everything,' he said. 'You heard one side of the conversation and are jumping to conclusions.'

'Oh, for God's sake!' Gabby was shrieking at him and couldn't seem to stop, her voice getting shriller with each word she threw at him. 'What sort of fool do you take me for? I heard you tell her about the takeover bid. *You're* the one behind it, aren't you? You were behind it the whole time and never let on. You let me make a complete and utter fool of myself that day when I came to you for help. All the while laughing behind my back at how you'd not only got the majority share of the St Clair Resort but me as a bonus.'

He looked as if he wanted to deny it, but at the last moment changed his mind. He shoved a hand through his hair again and, tossing his phone to one of the sofas, rubbed the back of his neck with his hand, as if to release the tension there.

'There are things you don't know that I was not at liberty to tell you,' he said, in a weighted tone.

'The truth is always a good place to start,' Gabby inserted coldly.

'The truth is, Gabriella…' Vinn paused, searching for the right words. 'I have been on a vendetta of sorts, but it really has nothing to do with you.'

She gave him a flinty glare. 'Oh, please,' she said. 'Don't let the highlights fool you, Vinn. I'm not really as blonde as I look.'

'I mean it, Gabriella,' he insisted. 'The person I have been targeting is no one you know, and I would like to keep it that way. He is not the sort of person I want anyone I care deeply about coming into contact with.'

She rolled her eyes in scorn. 'So you've decided you *do* actually care about me now, have you?' she asked. 'Why? Because I've caught you out? Or because I was surprisingly good in the sack?'

'Don't cheapen yourself like that,' Vinn said, his jaw so tight his teeth ached.

'I'm hardly what you could call cheap,' she

tossed back. 'Two point four million dollars is a heck of a lot of money to pay for sex. I hope you were happy with what you got, because that's all you're getting. It's over, Vinn.'

Vinn drew in a harsh breath. 'You would compromise your father's health just to spite me?'

Her eyes went wide with anger. 'You talk to me of compromising my father?' she spat. 'What gall you have! You've just done the dirtiest deed in business—swiping away his life's work behind his back.'

'It wasn't behind his back.'

Gabby stared at him, her mind reeling so much her head was starting to pound. 'W-what did you say?'

'Your father approached me about the takeover bid a couple of days before his heart attack,' he said. 'He suspected who was behind it, and he came to me for advice. I assured him I would do whatever I could to keep the St Clair Island Resort safe.'

Gabby opened and closed her mouth. Not able

to speak, hardly able to think. Her father had *known*? He had already approached Vinn for help? Then why…?

'Henry was well aware of the rumours going about, and he knew he couldn't raise the funds if a margin call was activated,' Vinn said. 'I had already helped him secure the house, and—'

Her eyes went wide as she choked, 'The house? You…you own my parents' *house*?'

He pushed his hand through his hair again. 'On paper, yes, but not on principle.'

She gave him a cynical glare. 'What is that supposed to mean?'

'It means I would never take their house from them, no matter how much money they owed me,' he said, holding her gaze.

Gabby struggled to contain her see-sawing emotions. There was so much she didn't know—*hadn't* known. She felt like a pawn in a chess game, moved about with no will or choice of her own.

'I am in no doubt that the stress of the business was what caused your father's heart attack,' Vinn continued. 'And then, of course, his worst night-mare actually did happen. The lenders suddenly wanted their money.'

Gabby swallowed a couple of times to clear her tight throat. 'So...so you had already agreed to help my father?' she said, still trying to make sense of it all.

'Of course I had,' he said. 'Your father stood by me when I was on the skids. He was the only one who ever believed I had potential. I found it hard, growing up without a father. My mother did her best, but I was heading down a pathway to disaster when your father took me aside and told me how it was up to me to turn it all around. He sponsored me through university and organised special coaching on campus to help with my dyslexia. There is no amount of money I wouldn't put out for him.'

'So...what you're saying is...the resort was never in any danger?' Gabby asked, frowning.

He met her questioning gaze without flinching. 'It was never in danger, Gabriella,' he said heavily. 'Your father is still the major share-holder, and as long as he wants to be he will remain so.'

She ran her tongue over her lips, surprised at how dry and cracked they felt. 'I'm not sure I am really following this…' she said. 'Why did you involve me? Why force me into marriage?'

He looked at her for a lengthy moment, his grey-blue eyes dark and unfathomable. 'I cannot think of a time when you were not a part of my dream for success,' he said. 'I have always wanted you. I can't explain it other than to say my life and my quest for success did not feel complete until I had you.'

'So I am some sort of status symbol, am I?' she asked churlishly. 'Like a top-model sports car to show the world you've really made it?'

'That is not quite how I would put it.'

She gave him another flinty look. 'How *would* you put it, Vinn?' she asked. 'You've already got a mistress. What on earth do you want with a wife—especially one like me?'

'I do not have a mistress,' he bit out. 'Do you really think I am that low?'

Gabby scored her fingernails into the soft bed of her palms. 'How can you stand there and lie to me like that?' she asked incredulously. 'I just heard you tell her you loved her.'

There was a long, tense silence.

Vinn let out his breath. 'All right,' he said. 'I will break my word to her and tell you.'

She arched her brows. 'What's this? A last-minute twinge of conscience, Vinn?'

He gritted his teeth and tried to be patient. 'The young woman I was talking to is not my mistress,' he said. 'She is my half-sister.'

She gave him another raised-brow look, which communicated cynicism along with disgust. 'Then why not clear up that little misunderstanding with the press?' she asked. 'Why go along with the story of her being your mystery lover?'

'I want to protect her,' he said. 'She doesn't have any idea of the sort of man her father is, or the lengths he will go to in order to keep his reputation intact.'

Gabby frowned. 'So...let me get this straight... this half-sister of yours is your father's child, not your mother's?'

'Of course she is not my mother's,' he said. 'My mother would have loved other children— she would have loved to have had a husband to bring them up with her. But the man she fell in love with was already married. He tricked her into a relationship, and then when she got pregnant put her out on the streets, threatening to destroy her if she ever told who the father of her child was. I only found out the day she died who he was. I will not rest until I bring him down for what he did to her.'

Gabby was having trouble following it all. 'Your father is a dangerous man?' she finally managed to ask.

His look was grim. 'Very,' he said. 'He has underworld connections—drugs, organised crime, that sort of thing. He found it amusing to try and swipe away your father's business because he found out about my connection to your family, but fortunately I have contacts who informed me of it so I could take evasive action.'

'Oh, Vinn…' she said. 'I don't know what to say… I feel so confused.'

He came up to her and held her by the shoulders, locking her gaze with the grey-blue intensity of his. 'Listen to me, Gabriella,' he said. 'I love you. I have loved you since the first day I set eyes on you, when you were fourteen and thinking yourself all grown up. I loved you when you *did* grow up. I even loved you when you married that scum Glendenning, because I felt deep down that one day we would be together.'

Gabby blinked back tears. 'Oh, darling, we would have been together so much earlier than this if I hadn't been too proud and stubborn to listen to you that night.'

'I blame myself,' Vinn said, dropping his hands from her shoulders as he began to pace the room. 'I handled it all wrong. I had not long landed back in the country when I heard Glendenning was playing around on you. I blame myself for Blair's death too. I should have seen that coming, but I didn't.'

Gabby shook her head and took a step towards him. 'No, no—you mustn't say that. It wasn't your fault. How can you think that?'

He gave her a grim look. 'Let me finish, *cara*, please,' he said, his voice rough with emotion. 'I was away too long. Blair had come to me for advice about his career before I left to take my mother home to Italy to die. He didn't want to take up a position in your father's business, but he was too afraid to admit it. He was ashamed of not being what your parents wanted him to be. He wanted to study art. He had a gift, a rare gift he should have felt free to explore, but he didn't want to let your parents down.'

'The painting in your foyer…' Gabby said, her heart swelling with pride and a host of other emotions she knew she would have to pick over later. 'Blair did it, didn't he?'

Vinn nodded. 'He was so talented, Gabriella. But he didn't believe in himself. I think that's why in the end he turned to drugs. He wanted to block out the insecurities he felt—the insecurities all of us feel at times. But for him they were like demons, gnawing away at him relentlessly. I tried to help him, and I felt I was making some headway, but then my mother was diagnosed with cancer. She desperately wanted to mend the rift she had made in her family by succumbing to my father's charm and having a child out of wedlock. I felt I owed it to her to take her home, to nurse her until the day she died. It seemed fitting. She was there at the moment I drew my first breath. I was there when she drew her last.'

Gabby stumbled towards him, wrapping her arms around him, loving him, adoring him, worshipping the man he was—the man he had always been.

'I can't tell you how much I love you,' she said. 'I am not worthy of you. I don't deserve your love. I think that's why I was so reluctant to believe you actually loved me. Deep down I know I don't deserve someone as wonderful as you. But somehow you have loved me through it all.'

Vinn tucked her in close, holding her against his heart. 'You do deserve to be loved, Gabriella,' he said. 'You are more than worthy of love, and no one could love you more than me. I am sure of it.'

She looked up at him with tears of happiness shining in her eyes. 'So the honeymoon is not quite over?'

He smiled and lifted her up in his arms. 'Just as soon as I carry you out of the house and back over the threshold it is going to get a second wind—so you had better prepare yourself for it.'

'I'm prepared,' Gabby said, shivering all over in anticipation. 'Or at least I think I am.'

He gave her a smouldering look. 'Let's put that to the test, shall we?' he said, as he carried her towards the door.

And not too much later Gabby passed with flying colours.